A PLACE REMOTE

# A Place Remote

*Stories*

## Gwen Goodkin

West Virginia University Press
Morgantown

Copyright © 2020 by West Virginia University Press
All rights reserved
First edition published 2020 by West Virginia University Press
Printed in the United States of America

ISBN
Paper 978-1-949199-61-1
Ebook 978-1-949199-62-8

Library of Congress Cataloging-in-Publication Data
Names: Goodkin, Gwen, author.
Title: A place remote : stories / Gwen Goodkin.
Description: First edition. | Morgantown : West Virginia University Press, 2020.
Identifiers: LCCN 2020008807 | ISBN 9781949199611 (paperback) |
      ISBN 9781949199628 (ebook)
Classification: LCC PS3607.O56367 A6 2020 | DDC 813/.6—dc23
LC record available at https://lccn.loc.gov/2020008807

Book and cover design by Than Saffel / WVU Press
Cover photo by Jan Schulz # Webdesigner Stuttgart on Unsplash

Stories in this collection previously appeared in the following publications:
"Winnie," *The Dublin Review*; "How to Hold It All In," *Atticus Review*; "Last
Chance," *Exposition Review*; "The Key," *The Carolina Quarterly*; "The Widow
Complex," *jmww*; "Waiver," *Black Fox Literary Magazine* as the winner of the
Black Fox Literary Magazine Contest; "Just Les Is Fine," *Fiction*; "A Month of
Summer," *Fixional*; "A Boy with Sense," *Reed Magazine* as the winner of the
John Steinbeck Award for Fiction

*For Jose*

# Contents

# Winnie

IT WAS the midnineties and I was headed to the same town as her on a job laying foundation. I'd met Gizzard at the Rusty Nail just before I shoved off. He's the one told me where she was.

"Oxford. Ain't that just north of Cincinnati?" he'd said. "You know Winnie Osterman's at the college there."

Winnie had that rare mix of dark hair and blue eyes, and a body that curved just right. She was dangerous, too. Put herself in the hospital once. All of us boys wanted to get close to her, pass a palm over her flame, but she was Benji's girl. Now word around town was they were through.

"I'll look her up," I said.

"I bet you will." He laughed, finished his beer. "Why don't you call her now?"

"You know same as me I don't have her number."

"Ask her mom."

I threw a five on the bar and let Royal know I was a goner. He gave me a nod. "See you at Christmas, Gizz," I said. "Probably in this same stool."

"If you're lucky," he said.

I hauled my trailer down to Oxford and unhitched at the state park. Back then, Boss had me bouncing around the country to places like Knoxville and Bismarck, even down into Mexico, chasing whatever concrete work a strip-mall developer threw at us. Campground life had become the norm. But after a long string of nights by myself, I found the park's lone pay phone and dialed.

"Winnie, it's RJ."

She took a second. "RJ?"

"Yeah," I said. "RJ Otto."

"Holy shit. This is a surprise." She laughed and my mind went to her bare neck. "How'd you get my number?"

"I called your mom." I pulled a book of matches from my pocket and lit one. "I thought I could bring over some beer."

"You're in Oxford right now?"

"Yeah," I said. "Here on a job."

"So you're bribing me with beer?" she said. "Want me to help find you a college girl."

"Something like that."

"I like it," she said. "Tonight's out, though. I have an exam tomorrow. But," she stopped to consider, "maybe Wednesday."

"Wednesday works," I said. "Tell me where you live and I'll be there at eight."

I had two nights to think. Ironed my best shirt. Made sure my jeans were clean and my jaw was smooth. Last time I shaved at night must have been high school. I picked up a twelve-pack on the way and brought cigarettes just in case. Sometimes she smoked, sometimes she didn't.

What I expected of a college was noise—music and shouts and the whoop-whoop of kids partying on their parents' dime. This one was quiet. Eerie. I held myself tight going up the dorm steps.

A handmade sign on her door said "Jessica and Winifred." No

one back home, not even the teachers, called her Winifred. I'd assumed she was just plain Winnie. The door was open so I knocked on the metal frame. I poked my head around the corner. No one was there. Girls passed and gave me curious looks. I checked my watch. 7:59.

"RJ." She walked toward me from the other end of the hall. Her long, dark hair flew with each step. *She must have a boyfriend*, was all I could think. *If not, these college assholes are dumber than dirt.*

We hugged. I thought she'd invite me in—I was standing in the doorway, half in, half out—but she put her toothbrush away and pulled a jacket from her closet.

"Let's go," she said.

"Where?"

"To a party." She stopped. "It's at a fraternity, so no outside guys. Don't worry, though, I'll sweet-talk them." She motioned for me to give her the twelve-pack. "We can't get caught by campus police. I have to be really careful because of my scholarship." She opened the box and stuffed some of the beers in her mini-fridge. She handed the box back to me bottom-heavy. "You'll have to carry it under your coat."

"I can drive," I said.

"It'll be a hassle to find parking," she said. "Let's just walk."

We talked about people from home. Who was getting married, which of those weddings were shotgun. Rumors of an affair between two teachers at school.

"Isn't it a pretty campus?" she said, looking up at the rooftops. All the buildings were light-red brick.

"Yeah," I said. "It's nice." The beer was digging into my rib. "Almost too perfect. Like it needs one of them oddball seventies spaceship buildings."

She wrinkled her nose. "No, I like that it's neat." She stopped and pointed. "See that small window high up?"

I tried to follow. "No."

She pulled me so close I knew what shampoo she used—the pink one that smelled like a Granny Smith. "There. That's where I study." We moved apart and started walking again. "You're the only one who knows where I hide. Don't you feel special?"

"Very." I lifted a pack of cigarettes from the inside pocket of my coat. "But why hide?"

"People think if they study with me, they'll get the same grades. They don't realize it doesn't work that way. Only I get the A."

"But what does it hurt to study next to them?"

"Because they don't want me to study with them. They want me to study for them. I can't afford to help anyone because of the scholarship. If I lose that, I'm over and out."

She asked me about work. I told her how it'd taken me to Mexico a couple times.

"Some days it's hotter'n a bitch and you're working full sun and you curse the place. Can't get the smell of fried corn and diesel smoke off you. Old ladies selling warm cheese, flies all over and people buying. Beyond belief." I pulled the plastic wrapper off the pack of cigarettes. "But I'll tell you what. I'm the first to raise my hand whenever a job down there comes up."

"Why?"

I saw a bench and set the beer down. "Soon as you cross the border, the tightness leaves your shoulders. Well—after you pass the guy with the machine gun." I fished some matches out of my coat. "The food's good. Real cheap, too. And, the women are nice." I shook out a cigarette.

"In bed?"

I lit the cigarette. "Hell no," I said. "Don't want 'em nice in bed."

Neither of us would look away. She smiled first, though.

"Want it?" I asked, holding the cigarette toward her.

"Like, yesterday," she said.

I lit another.

"Think you'll ever leave town for good?"

I shook my head. "All my friends are there."

"Guys are funny. They make friends in first grade and those are all the friends they need. Girls have about twelve different best friends in life."

We headed down a side street.

"Think you'll move back home?" I asked. We were at the bottom of the fraternity's porch steps. "Or leave for good?"

She dropped her cigarette and stepped on it. "I'm already gone, baby."

A guy leaned against the doorframe with his arms crossed. He wore big, loose jeans and a baseball cap. I couldn't see his eyes, he wore the hat so low. And there was a hoop earring through the brim. He'd actually thought that out.

"Hi, Jason," said Winnie. She gave him a big, slow hug and he pulled her close to his waist, all the while staring in my direction.

"Where's everybody else?" he asked.

"They'll be here soon," she said.

"Who's this?"

"This is RJ," she said. "He's my cousin. He's just here for a visit."

"Your cousin."

"Yeah," she said. "And look—we brought beer."

I pulled the box from my coat and offered it to him. He looked inside and pulled out three beers—he kept two for himself and gave one to Winnie.

"Come in," he said. "It's a ghost town right now. That'll change in an hour."

He moved over just enough for us to pass, then caught Winnie by the wrist. "I'll see you later," he said.

She flicked the brim of his hat. "Promise?" He had to take it off to set it back straight. He had small eyes set close together. Smart to keep them covered.

We walked toward what looked like a home library, all dark wood, fat armchairs, and navy carpet. "That guy at the door," she whispered. "His dad is the president of Ace Hardware or some shit." She took a gulp of beer. "He's loaded."

I looked around at the library with its dusty books and paisley wallpaper and wondered what the hell I was doing there.

"Most of the kids here are."

"Are what?"

"Loaded." She took another drink. "One of the girls I hang out with is from New York City and has a driver. Another has her own sailboat. I don't mean her family has a sailboat, I mean her family has a boat *and* she has her own sailboat." She finished her beer and waved at me for another.

I could tell she liked it in a way, being around all these people. Maybe she thought their money was going to rub off on her. I took the last two beers out of the box and flattened it.

"What's going on downstairs?" I asked.

"Nothing now," she said. "But there will be dancing."

"Hip hop?"

"What else is there to dance to?"

"Country."

She threw her head back and laughed. "Country music sucks. All that whining."

A couple girls passed the doorway, saw us, and kept walking. "Hip hop is all for show. It's like—cotton candy. Even the name—who's that guy? Puff Daddy? Hip hop looks big, but when you take a bite, it collapses and there's nothing to it but sugar. All you end up with is sticky fingers and filmy teeth." I lit two cigarettes. "Country is meat and potatoes."

"You can't have meat and potatoes all the time," she said. "People eat cotton candy because it's pretty and fun." She took a drag and blew smoke in my direction.

"You ever talk to Benji?"

"Never."

"You want to?"

"Nope," she said. "Over and done."

I ashed in my empty. "Got a boyfriend?"

"No boyfriend." She pressed her lips together.

"Why?"

"I was with one person all of high school," she said. "Not doing that again."

The door from the basement opened and the music flared. Then the door shut and it was only bass again. "Don't tell me you're sleeping around."

"I wouldn't call it sleeping." She raised her chin, ready to fight.

I took the bait. "Don't do that to yourself."

"You do it."

"Where you get that?"

We faced each other. She moved close enough to me to where I could smell the apple shampoo again. "Mexico."

Someone shouted "hey!" in an angry voice that made us flinch. Jason came toward us in big strides. "No smoking in the library."

Winnie and I looked at our cigarettes as if we'd never seen them before.

"Sorry, man." I dropped mine in the can. Winnie pushed hers in after.

He studied her, then me. "Intense conversation for a pair of cousins."

"We aren't cousins," I said.

"Oh, really," he said. "You're a tricky one, Winn." He turned to me. "How do you know Winn then?"

I laughed through my nose. Who was this guy? "Winnie and I go way back. Clear to kindergarten, ain't it?"

She nodded. The door opened and there was the music again, full volume.

"Are you going downstairs?" He pressed Winnie to his side and she hugged his waist and he picked her up like he was carrying her over the threshold and started toward the basement. She pretended to be annoyed, but I could see she loved it.

"Come on, RJ," she called over his shoulder.

"I think I'll head out." I wedged my empty into the corner of an armchair.

She told Jason to wait and he put her down. She came over to me. "You're leaving? We just got here. You haven't even met my friends."

"I gotta be up early."

"You should stay," she said. "I've got some cute friends." She raised her eyebrows.

"Thanks," I said. "But I'll leave you to your party." I gave her a tight hug and whispered in her ear. "He's hiding something with them big jeans," I said. "Enter at your own risk."

She covered a smile with her hand.

I didn't call her again. And after a month I damn near forgot about her. Then I heard a knock on the trailer door. I checked the TV to make sure it wasn't the show, then answered.

"Winnie Osterman," I said. "I'll be goddamned." There she stood, her hair shining in the moonlight, hands in her jacket pockets. "How'd you find me?" I waved her inside. She stepped up and looked around.

"Your truck was parked out front."

"But it's a new truck," I said.

"County's on the plate."

I turned down the TV and handed her a beer. She sat next to me on the bench around the table. Only place to sit really. We drank a bit. She took the cigarette I offered.

"You know what I'm going to ask."

She picked a piece of tobacco from her tongue. "I'm homesick is all."

"Next time call me," I said. "I'll pick you up. It's not safe to drive here by yourself at night. I even get spooked out here alone sometimes."

"I didn't drive here," she said. "My friend brought me." She pushed off her shoes. "She told me I was crazy and didn't want to leave me here, but I made her go when I saw your light on."

"Is she picking you up? I can drive you."

"I didn't ask her to come back."

Sounded like an open-ended plan to me. We traded bits of gossip about people from home. Friends breaking up. Car accidents. People who'd quit school to work out at the plant.

Then she said, "RJ, why'd you call me last month?"

I shrugged, "Homesick is all."

We both smiled.

"Anyone ever tell you how pretty you are?"

She plucked the tab on her beer can. "Once or twice."

I kissed her, slow at first, then we couldn't get rid of our clothes fast enough.

"I have bad news." I pointed at the bed. "The sheets are outside drying."

She laughed and I went outside pecker swinging. I didn't care. No one to see me anyway. I put them sheets on in record time. She was on top of me and I couldn't stop touching her skin. "Winnie," I said into her hair. "Winnie."

"I got milk and cereal," I said when she woke up. "But I buy my coffee at the gas station."

"Gas station coffee is fine with me," she said.

"Come on, get dressed."

She propped herself up on an elbow. "You can't go alone?"

"I can," I said. "But I don't want to."

And then we kissed and I ran my fingertips clear down to the bottom of her spine and past it, to the back of her soft thighs until she shivered on top of me.

"I mean it this time," I said. "I got to get to a phone."

"Why?"

"To call in to work." I lit a cigarette and pulled on my jeans.

"I have class," she said. "I have to go back."

"Don't do that. You can skip it once, right?"

She pulled her hair into a ponytail, said nothing.

"Let's get a real breakfast." I said. "Eggs and bacon."

After we ate, she wanted to go to her dorm to shower and brush her teeth.

"You can shower at my place," I said.

"But I need to brush my teeth," she said. "And change my clothes."

"I'll stop and get you a toothbrush." I spotted a gas station nearby and pulled in. "And you look real good in the clothes you're wearing."

"I need clean underwear."

"Skip the underwear."

She pulled out her ponytail and redid it. "You just don't want me to go back to school."

"Correct."

"Why?"

"Who'd let a pretty girl like you out of his sight?" I offered her my hand. She stared at it. "Come on now." She took my hand and scooted across the bench seat.

When I stepped out of the shower, she was combing her wet hair with her fingers and still wrapped in a towel. That came off real quick.

She was on my lone pillow. I'd bunched up a sweatshirt for myself. Our legs were together. She rubbed the calluses at the base of my fingers.

"What's it like?" she said. "Your job."

"Sometimes at the end of the day, my hands feel like they're cased in concrete. All the dust on them hardens and I want my fingers to move, but they're molded in place," I said. "First thing tomorrow and clear till the end of the day I'll catch hell for missing work. We're already behind schedule and the customer's laying into us for starting late on account of all the water we hit when we dug the footings. Now we got to put antifreeze in the concrete because we're up against winter. This is all boring to you."

She turned my hand over and studied it. "I like to hear you talk," she said. "Makes me feel like I'm sitting in front of a fire." She ran a finger across my palm.

I flinched. "Tickles."

She did it again. I held my hand steady and stared at her.

"What's the J in your name stand for?" she asked. "James?"

I felt the stubble above my lip. I needed to shave. "J is for Junior. Though my pop wishes he'da saved that for my brother."

"Oh, you can't mean that," she said and kissed a callus.

"Sure as shit I do," I said. "He tells me every chance he gets."

She stretched the sheet tight over her legs and tucked it deep under her thighs. "Dads," she said. "Can't live with 'em, can't live without 'em."

"I don't know what you're talking about," I said. "From what I can tell, you won the dad lottery." I pushed my fingers between hers. "When I think about your dad, I picture him mowing the lawn in his German hat, smoking his pipe. He seems like a pretty happy-go-lucky guy."

She pulled her fingers free of mine. "He sure has you fooled."

I didn't know what to do—leave it at that or ask her to explain. Looking back, I wish I'd stood up, got dressed, and convinced her to walk the campground with me. Changed the scenery.

She jumped out of bed and started putting her clothes on. "Everyone in town thinks he's such a nice guy," she said. "And they'll never think anything different because they don't want to. That's how it is."

I tried to get close to her but she pushed me away. "What do you want them to think?"

"I want them to *know*."

"Know what?"

"What he did to me."

She stopped bumping around the room and stared at me, flushed, breathing hard. I waited. If she wanted to say something, tell me whatever it was, I gave her the chance. She turned away from me and kept quiet.

I walked to the fridge and poured her a glass of milk. She drank some. Neither of us spoke. I pulled on some shorts, turned on the TV, and let her come to me. She did eventually and things between us were more careful, like we were setting the table with the good dishes.

"So, then—what is your middle name?" She took a sip of milk.

"Christopher," I said.

"RC," she said. "Like the drink."

"Yep."

"That'll be my nickname for you," she said. "Cola."

I turned one of her wrists over, ran my thumb across the soft side, and felt two vertical scars. I stared at them.

"If you cut the length of each vein, you bleed more," she said.

"How did you even know to do that?"

She finished the last of her milk. "You can find out anything if you want to."

When I woke in the morning, she was gone. I found a note in the kitchen that said, "Goodbye, Cola." I threw on my jeans and jumped in the truck. She couldn't have walked. It was too far. I drove slow and searched the side of the road. I parked in the first space I saw at the dorm and thought for a while about what to do. I went to the front door and waited for someone to come out. Last time, I'd only been locked out a few seconds. This time it felt like minutes. I nodded a thank-you to the guy who let me in and took the steps two at a time. When I reached her door, I went to knock but stopped short when I heard her voice. I stood there, unsure of what to do. I didn't know it then, but I realize now that if I knocked on the door, she'd have to face the very thing she was hiding, that home had come to her, in spite of how hard she'd worked to cover it up. I had enough sense to understand she wanted space between us, so I took a step back, then another, and I turned around and headed for the stairs.

I found Gizzard just where I left him. "Tell me you've been home once or twice since I saw you last," I said. We slapped each other's shoulders and I settled into my stool. We shot the shit for a while and then he asked: "Did you call?"

I lit my cigarette. "Bet your ass I did."

He was surprised. "And?"

"And I brought her some beer."

"That's it?"

"Mostly," I said.

"What do you mean, 'mostly?' " He raised his eyebrows.

If I told him, he'd expect details—what happened, what I'd done wrong. I didn't want to get into it, so I gave him the minimum. "Met her at her dorm, went to a party, left."

"Together?"

"Separate."

"You're a chump then," he said. "How do you blow a chance like that?"

I lifted off my seat to get a view of the back. "Have you seen her?"

"Nope." He raised his empty at Royal. "You," he said, pushing his middle finger between my top ribs, "fucked up."

Just after the new year I was hitching my trailer to my truck out back at Mom and Dad's. It was so cold I had to talk myself into touching the metal winch.

"RJ."

That made me jump. I banged my knee against the winch and yelped in pain. There she stood, covering a laugh.

"Winnie." I caught my breath. "That ain't funny."

"I'm sorry," she said, still laughing.

I rubbed my knee then shook it out. "I'm going to start calling you The Magician. Never know where you'll appear," I said. "Or disappear."

She stared at the frozen mud, then eventually met my eyes. "Can I explain?"

"You don't need to," I said. "Want to go inside? It's easier to talk when your teeth aren't chattering."

She shook her head and jammed her hands in her coat pockets. "You don't know what it's like down there. All those rich kids. I do

what I can to fit, but I'm not one of them. And it seems like—"
She lifted her face toward the gray clouds. "The harder I try, the
plainer it gets: I'm somewhere I don't belong."

My fingers were going numb. "Then stop trying."

She sighed. "It's my only way out."

I pointed a thumb at the trailer. "I'm nearly ready to go." The
snow had started, a flake or two at a time. "You could come with
me. Leave the snow for the sunshine. And peaches. Lots of them
in Georgia."

She backed away. "I can't."

"Just drive down with me. If you don't like it, I'll take you back
to school."

"No," she said. "I can't."

I left town and didn't go back for a long time. I needed to get away,
give myself a chance to decide who to be and where to be it. After
I finished the Georgia job, I jumped at a gig down in Chihuahua.
Found work with an American putting up apartment buildings.
Finally I caved to Mom and agreed to come home for Christmas
after three years away. I brought my girlfriend, Lorena, home with
me. I'd met her soon after I moved to Chihuahua and we'd been
dating ever since.

We went to the Rusty Nail and I opened the door expecting
to see Gizzard front and center, but his seat was empty. I searched
the bar and spotted him at the pool table. We went up to him and
I gave him a slap on the back.

"Hey, Gizz," I said. "Meet my girl." I had my arm around Lorena's shoulders, proud of how pretty she was. Her and Gizzard
shook hands. Then he said, "Lorena, this is my wife, Winnie."

I hadn't recognized her. She'd puffed up, cut off her hair, and
put some skunk-looking stripes in it.

"Winnie Osterman?" I said, still not believing. "What happened to your hair?"

She laughed. "I take it you don't like it."

"You guys are married? When'd that happen?"

"Two months ago," said Gizzard. He pulled her close.

She shook her can and finished the last drink. "I came to the bar a few years back, couple days after New Year's. I'd gone to your parents' and your mom said you'd just left but you might have stopped here on your way out." She looked at me, then away. "And there was Gizzard."

I clapped Gizz on the shoulder. "Well, bud," I said. "I wouldn't've put money on it, but"—I needed a second before I could get it out—"congratulations."

"You, too, Cola," Winnie said and nodded at Lorena, who was talking to Benji's latest model-type girlfriend. Benji and me greeted each other with a nod.

"Cola?" said Gizzard.

"Old joke," I said, embarrassed for her—reaching for something that wasn't there. I changed the subject. "Where you putting that fancy degree to use?"

"Oh, no degree," she said. "I dropped out." Gizzard kept her close enough that she had to lean my way to be heard. "I'm a teller at the bank."

"Teller's a good job," I said. "But why quit school?"

She finished her beer and handed her empty to Gizz. "Got to be too much," she said. "All the back and forth."

Gizz left to get another round.

"I never told him about us," I said to her.

"I know," she said.

"I never told him nothing."

Not long after I ran into Winnie and Gizzard at the Rusty Nail, the plant shut its doors and left for Mexico. People wanted their TVs big as couches and dirt cheap and they couldn't have both with American labor. The Rusty Nail eventually closed down. A trinket shop took its place, selling greeting cards and teddy bears.

I've been in Dallas nearly a decade now, running my own construction business and raising a family. I don't get back to town much. Whenever Mom gets me on the phone, which isn't often I'm ashamed to say, she tells me all the gossip.

"That classmate of yours, the Osterman girl—what's her name?"

"Winnie." I'm talking to Mom while I'm in the garage, squeezing wood glue on a split picture frame.

"Yeah, well. She made manager at the bank," says Mom. "Now that she's a big shot, they had to run out and buy Louie Croy's house." Mom blows on her coffee and takes a sip. "Poor old Croy wasn't even cold in the grave before that son of his had the house for sale."

I grab an old cloth to clean up the glue drips. "Sounds about right," I say.

"You know what house I'm talking about."

"Sure," I say, though I can't recall it.

"Wonder what Greg thinks." She refuses to call him Gizzard.

Lorena opens the door from the kitchen and waves me inside for dinner. "What he thinks about what?"

"Why," says Mom, "about living right aside her parents."

I remember—the end of my conversation with Winnie. After I told her Gizzard didn't know anything about us—or her—a country song came on.

"I love this song," she said.

"Wait—you told me you *hated* country music."

"When did I say that?"

"At that terrible party we went to at your school."

"Oh. Well," she said. "People change."

"Or maybe they just go back to who they really are." She didn't like that, but shrugged it off.

"I started listening to rap after I left Oxford."

"You? RJ Otto. Listen to hip hop."

"No," I said. "I listen to rap."

"Same difference."

"Big difference," I said. "Only the classics, though. Dre. Cube. Public Enemy. Tribe. NWA."

"How'd that happen?"

"You told me music should be fun," I said. "So I gave it a try."

She sang the country song again.

"You know this is 'Cadillac Ranch,' " I said. "Springsteen wrote it."

"Springsteen sucks," she said, then laughed.

"Blasphemy," I said.

She went back to singing.

"Sounds like he's talking about the pool stick he wishes he had," I pointed to the cues lined up on the wall next to the pool table. We cracked up and there it was, the moment she'd been reaching for.

She held her hands about a foot apart and sang in my ear.

I forced a smile. The moment was over. "It's really about a hearse," I said.

"What?" she yelled at me. The music was loud and Winnie was dancing backwards toward Gizzard.

"The song!" I shouted. "It's about a hearse!"

I don't know if she heard me, though. She'd pushed open a space for herself that was already filled in by the crowd.

# A Boy with Sense

CHELSEA AND me are on our way to Gram and Poppy's for one of our weekend visits. I'm excited because we haven't seen them in a while and I've been wondering about the crops and the herd. As it is now, I only see Dad and Gram and Poppy at the farm every other weekend. In between, I live at Mom's and go to school. I don't care much about school, but Mom says too damn bad. You'll learn to love it.

She's wrong, though. Farming's what I love. What I'm best at.

Mom can think what she wants. I'd stay at the farm for good. Never come back, if she'd let me. But I know better than to tell her that.

Chelsea gripes that the farm's dirty, that Gram doesn't use soap in the dishwasher and lets the cats eat off the plates. But, really, she says all this for Mom's sake.

"Best day of my life," Mom says with a cigarette between her lips, "was the day I left that shithole and that man-baby of a husband. Couldn't handle that I gave you two more attention than I gave him. What did he expect? You were both so little."

Here we go again. I steal a look at Chelsea, but she keeps her eyes on the empty fields that stretch for miles beyond our back-seat windows.

Mom blows smoke at the ceiling.

"The big baby had to go find someone else to cuddle him." She flicks ash through the window crack. "Mimi." Mom points at the windshield with her cigarette. "What a catch. On both sides." Mom lets out a sharp laugh and shakes her head no.

We're almost there—I can tell by the sweet, grassy smell of cow manure that fills the car. Mom and Chelsea trade more complaints. Chelsea plugs her nose. I like the smell so I ignore them and keep to myself. Further down the road, Gram and Poppy's neighbor Bud has a pig farm. His farm stinks bad, not sweet at all, just sour and salty and dead.

Soon as the car's parked in the drive, Mom pushes unlock and I fling open my door. No cows in the front pasture, so I sprint along the mud path to the back, past the milking shed. I remember not to scare the herd and slow to a walk. The cows act like they don't notice me, but I see their eyes turn my way. They stay in place, working their jaws. All except Pep. She trots toward me, pulled into the mud by her own weight.

First time Poppy caught me whispering secrets in Pep's ear, his eyes went hard.

"Don't pick no favorites, son," he warned.

I stared back at him, kept my mouth shut. Knew better than to tell him that he had it all wrong. That she's the one did all the choosing.

One day last summer I rode with Dad on the four-wheeler to round up the cows. He dropped me at a group and told me to get them moving with the switch. When I walked toward them clicking my tongue, the group scattered. Only Pep stayed put. I swatted her rump to get her going, but she stood quiet and still. Her eyes waited for me, so I reached for her on my toes and wrapped my arm under her jaw. Even when I pressed my cheek on hers, she didn't move.

So like I said. She picked me.

I run to the fence and unhook the electric wire. I have to jump on the middle rail to reach the top of Pep's snout. When I pet her, she quits chewing, pushes her nose against my hand, and closes her eyes. Dad claims he's never laid eyes on a heifer like her—all black except for a crooked white line running from her neck to the bottom of her rib cage, like a skunk. I called her Pepe at first for Pepé Le Pew, but that sounded like a boy name, so I shortened it to Pep.

I give her a firm pat and hurry to Gram for a hug.

"If you're going to help milk, best get a move on." Gram steers me toward the milking shed. I break into a jog.

"Don't go wandering around with no jacket!" shouts Mom. "Hear me?"

I wave to her over my shoulder. Dad and Poppy are talking, arms crossed, inside the milking shed. Next to Dad, Poppy seems shorter than he already is. It isn't until I stand close to Poppy that I remember he's taller than me.

"Cows about to come in?" I ask.

"Yeahp," says Dad. He lifts me high so I can see the pens from above. They look cold and hushed without the cows.

Dad sets me on the cement floor between the two sets of stalls.

"Ready to clean, son?" Poppy asks.

"Yeahp," I say.

Dad brings in the heifers four at a time on each side. Cows' hooves covered in mud and manure tread heavy on the cement. Their pink spotted udders are so tight with milk that the veins look like they could bust.

I get to work wiping clean the udders. Poppy attaches a set of milkers on one of the new cows just bought from a farm on the other side of Mansfield. I know she's new 'cause the tag in her ear is yellow. Dad says the farmer had to sell off his stock because he couldn't keep up with the big operations moving in. Seems like every month another farm's on the block. With sixty-five head and the corn, wheat and soybeans on top of that, Dad thinks we have as much as we can handle.

"Well, son, what do you reckon?" Poppy asks. "Ready to help bale next year?" He's walking down the line, stopping at each stall.

"No," I say. "This year."

"Not until you eat something other'n that junk food," says Dad. His voice is deep—almost as low as the cows.

"I cleared my plate last night."

Poppy takes off his hat, combs his sweaty hair, and puts the hat back in place.

"Boy's still not eating meat?"

He's looking at Dad, not me.

"Seems like he's getting plenty of carrots, though." Dad grins and messes my hair. I cross my arms, lean away from him. I've heard enough jokes about my orange hair. "Calm down," says Dad.

"You aren't paying your cow any attention." Poppy lifts a bored finger toward Pep.

I have to stand on my toes to reach her back teat. Just after I fix the metal tube on her, a pool of white collects in the small see-through tank below. Her body tenses. She's talking to me now. Happy to be relieved of all that milk.

"Stay clear of her hoof, son." Poppy blows his nose, then pushes the handkerchief deep in his back pocket.

The constant hiss and shunk of the milking machines puts me

in a trance. Dad and Poppy's low voices, as they gossip or complain about the price of things, makes me nearly fall asleep. Hooves scraping cement bring me back to attention, though. So does the cows' talk.

"Last one," says Dad. He leads the group out while Poppy hoses down the cement floor. I switch on the cleaning system. In the pump room, Poppy gives me a taste of the milk out of the metal tank. It's warm and full of bubbles—thicker on my tongue than the milk at Mom's.

"Go for a ride?" Dad asks once we're outdoors.

"I guess," I say. Don't want to seem too excited.

"We'll have to drive a bit to get to hard ground," says Dad.

"I don't mind."

"We can go down the dirt road or around the pond," he says, swinging his leg over top of the four-wheeler's seat.

"Dirt road."

Soon as I grab hold of his belt, Dad guns it. Cool wind strokes my face. After a while the air stings my cheeks, but I ignore it.

Trees grow so thick on both sides of the dirt road that they create a sort of tunnel. Underneath that sky of leaves, daytime stops. We enter the sunshine again and I breathe deep. I feel like I'm floating at the top of a swimming pool, staring at the clouds. The dirt road dead ends into a pasture where fingers of tall grass skim my ankles. We follow the rise and fall of the hills. The air catches my laughter, carries it away.

"Let's quick check the winter wheat," Dad says over his shoulder. "You drive so I can get a good look."

We switch and I drive until he taps me on the side and points. He climbs off the four-wheeler, sets one knee in the dirt.

"Looks good." He pushes himself to full height from the ground and searches the sky. "I expect it'll snow soon."

I bet he can guess the exact hour.

"Do you want it to?"

"Next week would be best. Give the wheat a little extra time." He waves me toward him and I sit in the space he makes behind him on the seat.

Just in front of Gram and Poppy's kitchen door, Dad bucks the four-wheeler to a stop. We walk inside. I catch heat from Chelsea's glare.

Gram's got dinner ready to go.

"Almost started eating without you," she says. Poppy's already serving himself sauerkraut, ham, and potatoes.

Chelsea won't touch anything but the potatoes. I serve myself a heap. Mom never makes food like this. I can only get it here. Dinner at the farm is serious business. We don't talk much. Just get to work on our plates. There's no room for waste at the farm, even when it comes to talking. Don't waste words—or time.

After dinner and dishes, Dad says, "Carter? Chelsea? Let's play a game."

Chelsea fetches a board game from the hall closet and I take a chair at the table.

"Get the career cards in a pile," she says to me.

They're scattered everywhere—Doctor, Lawyer, Accountant, Teacher.

"How's come there's no Farmer card?" I fan the stack again in case I missed it.

"They know you'd lose for sure if you pick that one." Dad laughs quick and sharp.

"Then I'm not playing." I drop the cards and cross my arms.

"You'll play," says Dad, slapping a plastic game piece in front of me.

"Keep acting like a baby, we'll get your pacifier out of the cupboard," says Chelsea. She's soaking up Dad's favor.

"As long as you bring your witch costume with you," I say, trying not to smile.

"Knock it off," says Dad. He shoves a blue plastic pin in one of the holes of my miniature red car and spins the wheel. "You know, I could have been a linebacker for Ohio State." His eyes dart side to side. Every time he tells this story, he likes to pause, make sure the whole room's listening.

I play along, let him know I'm listening. *Tell me*, I say with my eyes. *I want to hear.*

With one loud laugh, Poppy cuts the silence. Chelsea and me look at him, then each other.

"Don't lie to your kids, son." He tosses a section of newspaper on the countertop. "That scout come once and told you 'Thanks, but no thanks.' "

Dad and him are acting like they're telling jokes. Laughing at each other.

"How would you know what that scout said?" Dad laughs, but I can hear tightness in it. "Did he talk to you?"

"Didn't say a word," says Poppy. "And that told you everything."

"I wonder," Dad says. "How much did you pay him to pass on me?"

Poppy wraps his folded hands around the back of his head.

"I paid him what you're worth." He leans back in his chair. "Nothing."

"You would say that." Dad stands and leaves the room. Goes to the coat hooks, picks up his jacket, and walks out. The screen door takes its time shutting, but when it does, it's so quiet we hear the click.

My room at Gram and Poppy's is Dad's old room, close to the kitchen. I open my eyes to darkness and the sound of dishes clinking. I dress quick as I can and go to the kitchen.

"There's cereal," Gram says. Her back's to me. "Or you can make yourself some toast."

"You think Dad and Poppy want my help?"

She grabs a plate and runs the towel along the edge, one hand following close after the other. When that plate's finished, she wipes two more. Her whole body shakes drying the dishes.

"Eat something and go on then."

I scarf down four big bites of cereal, pull on my green work boots, and run out the door, down the wide mud path to the shed. A bright spotlight shows me the entry. Full of impatience, an occasional cow raises her voice.

When I enter the shed, I hear Poppy talking.

"He'da never done none of this with Bridget."

Poppy doesn't see me, but I have a clear view of him and Bud.

Bud says "Yeahp" slow. He grunts, adjusts the blue waistband that hugs the curve of his round belly.

"That's one thing I'll say about Bridget. She ran a tight ship." Poppy reads the gauge on the wall. "Now he wants to spend his mornings laying around drunk with that lazy no-good."

So that's where Dad is. With Mimi.

I count to five and walk to where they can see me.

"Need help?" I ask.

Poppy looks at Bud, then me.

"Suppose so," he says.


After we finish milking the last group, Poppy invites Bud inside for bacon and eggs—it's no trouble, Evelyn can make extra—but Bud says he has to tend to his hogs. Poppy digs in his pocket while Bud stares at the wet ground. At last Poppy finds the stack of folded dollars. He slips them into Bud's hand.

"I like cows better," I say when I hear Bud's engine rev.

"Better'n what?"

"Hogs." With my head, I point at the door Bud just left. "Cows smell nicer. And they sound soft and low, not screaming in your ear like hogs."

Poppy nods.

"Them cows need to be up front." Poppy leaves the milking shed, makes me hurry to catch him. He's short and skinny and moves fast for a grandpa. "It's all mud in the back. You open the fence and I'll keep 'em tight with the four-wheeler."

Our feet sink into the mud that leads to the back pasture, beyond the old red barn where we store the hay. Gram's cats run wild in that barn. I don't dare go in. But, Chelsea? That's her favorite spot.

Just like I figured, Pep's up front. I disconnect the electric fence and hop on the middle rail.

"Hey, let's get going," says Poppy, shooing me like a fly. He hands me a switch pulled from the side of the milk shed.

I quick pat Pep on the top of her nose and begin to open the gate.

"Son!" yells Poppy. "You know better'n to let 'em out 'fore I'm ready."

"Sorry," I mumble to the ground.

Poppy starts the engine, drives slow till he's just in front of the cat barn. Over his shoulder he yells "Okay!" and I open the gate.

Halfway through Pep stops. I know she's waiting for me, but she's holding up all the other cows, too.

"Go, Pep," I tell her, but she stays put. I look at Poppy. He's staring at us expecting the herd.

"Go!"

She won't budge. With all the weight I can muster, I lean on her hip bone. Only her tail moves. The rough, wet hairs graze my cheek. They leave behind a slash of manure that burns my skin. I wipe my face clean with my jacket cuff.

Poppy drives back toward us. With a jolt he stops the four-wheeler and slides off the seat. I can't tell who's going to get it—me or Pep. He's coming at us fast and I want to run, but know better. Stare fixed on me, Poppy raises his arm. I shut my eyes and crouch into the fence.

The whip-crack of his hand on flesh makes me flinch. I open my eyes and realize it was Pep he hit, not me. My girl heaves herself forward, does her best to move through the gate. I bite my lip till I taste blood. Better to bleed than cry.

"What the hell is wrong with you? Get them cows moving!"

I lean over the edge of the fence to hide my red face and tap the cows with the switch, telling them, "Go on now." From the corner of my eye, I catch Poppy glaring at me with his mouth in a straight line.

By now most of the cows are in between the back and front pasture. Poppy's on the four-wheeler keeping them in line. I let my eyes wander to Dad's house. It sits opposite Gram and Poppy's front door, on the other side of the back pasture.

Before I have time to think, I jump overtop the fence. Round the tail end of the herd, I run toward Dad's house fast as my boots will allow. I try to avoid the piles of manure, but they look like mud and my boots get sucked in. I stop, search the distance for Poppy. He's nowhere in sight.

At Dad's back door, I nearly step inside when, last second, I remember to take off my boots. I lean on the butter-yellow siding to wrench them off. The kitchen is messy with empty cartons piled on the countertops, beer cans, and a sink full of dirty dishes. I sneak toward the back bedroom where Dad and Mimi sleep. I hear Dad snoring and peek through the door. All I see above the blanket is the white frizz of Mimi's hair. Slow and steady I tiptoe to his side of the bed.

"Dad," I whisper in his face.

He opens his eyes wide, stares at me.

"We finished the morning chores," I say, proud to include myself.

Mimi props herself up on her elbow and all I can do is stare at her bare chest. She reaches for a pack of cigarettes on the nightstand, doesn't care if I see her naked.

"Guess you missed chores then." She lights her cigarette. "About fucking time."

Dad throws off the covers and sits on the edge of the bed. Except for his white underwear, he's naked. Wiry brown-gray hair covers his skin—between knuckles, around nipples, springing off his thighs.

"Poppy's going to be mad at me. I ran here before we finished moving the cows."

Dad wipes his eyes. He tries to get up but hits the wall. Stumbles back onto the mattress.

"Get out of here. Turn on some cartoons," he points over his shoulder with his thumb. "I'll be out in a minute."

I leave Dad and switch on the TV in the family room. After a whole cartoon, start to finish, I'm hungry—don't want to wait on him another minute. I creep back to the bedroom to ask if he's ready, but him and Mimi are under the covers again and I know better than to go in. I find my boots. Leave through the front door. This time I walk the long way to Gram and Poppy's, on the road.

Gram slides open the window.

"Where *was* you?"

I shrug my shoulders.

"Went for a walk."

"A *walk*?" I could have told her I dug a hole to China and she'd have sounded the same. Like she's never heard such a stupid idea.

"Poppy is fit to be tied," she says. The window slams shut.

Makes me jump. I'm scared Poppy has the belt waiting. I imagine it's wrapped tight around his fist, buckle hanging. He doesn't do it often, but when he does—

I take my time and act like nothing once I'm in the kitchen. At the table Poppy sits drinking coffee. He shakes his head at me and laughs, but not like he thinks I'm funny. More like he thinks I'm a boy with no sense.

"A walk," he says, still smiling and shaking his head.

"Leave the boy be," says Gram.

I ignore them, make my way through the kitchen, back to Dad's old bedroom.


We've had snow too many times to count since Dad and me checked the fields on the four-wheeler. Christmas came and went without us seeing him. Now it's almost Easter and I really need to know if he got the cover he wanted for the winter wheat. Sitting around all day, every day in school means I miss out on learning what's important—what's going on at the farm.

Like, a good corn crop is always knee high by the fourth of July. Everyone knows that, though. What they don't know is a cow has to be milked twice a day, else her milk goes bad. Don't scare a cow, 'cause you might scare the milk clear out of her—dry her up for good. No milk and she'll be sold for slaughter.

Every morning, I pray that Mom will tell us to get our farm clothes packed. I wait with the front door open, hoping she'll tell us she forgot. But she just yells at me to shut the goddamn door and quit letting in the flies.

Warm weather gets me thinking about farm chores, wondering if I'll be able to handle a bale of hay. So before I start homework, I sneak down to the basement and find Mom's ankle weights. This summer I'm not going to miss out on baling. I lift the flat, heavy beanbags until my muscles feel like rubber. I set the weights on the cement ground, take the stairs two at a time. Soon as I open the basement door, Mom rushes past, pulling a breeze with her.

"Chelsea!" she yells. Before I get in trouble for nothing, I creep out of the kitchen.

"Come back here, Carter. This concerns you, too."

"Great," I whisper.

Chelsea and me sit in our usual seats across from each other at the kitchen table. Mom searches her purse, pulls out a cigarette.

"Your dad was in jail." Mom's lighter snaps a tall flame in front of her cigarette. She tilts her head and inhales deep. A stream of smoke rushes out of her mouth.

Chelsea puts her chin on the table and stares straight through me. I think she looks funny—like a head with no body.

The laughs build in my chest until I can't hold them back anymore. They rush out faster than my stomach can keep up. I gasp for breath. Mom doesn't tell me to shut my mouth like I expect her to. She runs her cigarette under the faucet and throws it in the garbage.

"Way your Gram tells it, Mimi called the cops. Claimed your dad punched a hole through the wall—and then went for her." Mom bites the skin next to her thumbnail. "She's a liar. He was never violent like that with me."

Tears make two lines on Chelsea's face, connecting her eyes to her lips. I have to cover my mouth just to keep in the giggles. My sister looks like a floating head.

From behind Chelsea's chair, Mom hugs her and whispers in her ear. Chelsea doesn't hug her back.

Mom stands up, takes a deep breath.

"Carter." Her voice cracks.

Now I'm going to catch it for laughing.

"Poppy had to sell the cows."

I can't stop the giggles. With both hands, I cover my mouth.

She walks over to my side of the kitchen table and kneels next to me so her face is close to mine. "Poppy sold the cows."

I press my lips together as tight as I can and put my forehead on the table. A tear slides past my shut lips, drops to the floor.

"Gram said your dad hasn't helped Poppy in months. He couldn't run the farm on his own anymore and Bud can only fill in so much."

I want to yell at her. Tell her it's her fault Poppy sold the cows. If she would've let me live on the farm, everything would be the same as always.

"I could have helped," I say to the floor.

"I know," says Mom. "But Poppy needs your dad." She's staring at me even though I won't look at her.

"Can I leave?" asks Chelsea.

"The reason I called Gram is because Beth needs me to cover her shift on Saturday—"

"No!" screams Chelsea.

"And I can't afford a sitter."

Chelsea jumps out of her chair. It tips backwards, hits the floor.

"You're going," says Mom steady.

"Oh no I'm not," says Chelsea. She stomps out of the kitchen, all the way upstairs.

"I want to go," I tell Mom. I lift my head off the table and look straight at her.

"I know you do." With her thumb, she wipes the tear from my cheek. Tells me that she's dropping us off at Gram and Poppy's Saturday morning, that we're staying overnight. I run upstairs and yell the news through Chelsea's door. She lands on her bed with a thud and screams.

The closer we drive to the farm, the harder Chelsea kicks me. Even though I see her shoe coming, the pain takes me by surprise. She shoves me against the door with both feet.

"Farm boy." Spit arcs from her lips to the floor. I'd like to say she feels bad about the hurt, but she's grinning so big her teeth show. She wants to leave me with bruises, so as I don't forget who's boss. But I won't say uncle.

"Quit kicking your brother!" Mom yells at Chelsea. I meet Mom's eyes in the rearview mirror. From her squint, I see she thinks I'm as much to blame.

The fields leading to Gram and Poppy's are quiet, just sprouting their next crop. I miss rows of green cornstalks flashing so quick past the window the car can't keep up.

We're close enough to see the front pasture.

Empty.

My chest gets hot and full of air. I shove my foot under Mom's seat and push it so far to the front that I have to hold myself on the back seat with my elbows.

Soon as we park next to Gram and Poppy's front door, I see her. She's waiting for me like usual. I'm ready to jump out the door before the car stops.

"Pep!" I yell and run to the fence. Her body tenses. She cries loud and deep. When I reach for her nose, she moves it away from my hand. I try again, but still she avoids me. I can wait, so I cross my arms, hold onto the fence with my elbows.

After a while I try again and bring my hand close to her nose. This time she doesn't move, quits chewing.

"Carter," Mom calls to me. "Come say hi to your Gram."

Mom and Gram sound like they're telling each other secrets, so Chelsea and me head inside. We fight to be the first one through the screen door. Chelsea beats me with a kick to the shin. I refuse to cry, so I press where her heel hit and breathe deep.

Chelsea walks slow through the kitchen toward the family room. I let go of my leg and follow her. Dad's asleep on the couch. He's snoring loud. I can't get over his fat, red face.

"I thought he was in jail," I whisper to Chelsea.

"What part of 'was' don't you get?" she asks. Her eyes are mean.

We wait in the doorway between the kitchen and family room. Chelsea studies the brown speckled carpet. Warm weather brings in the fleas, so I know she won't sit on the floor.

"I'm bored," says Chelsea. "Let's play a game." Her long brown hair follows her into the hallway.

"Which one?" I ask.

She doesn't bother to answer. I know it's best to let Dad sleep. Summer's coming, so him and Poppy are real tired at the end of the day. But it's just after lunch. He shouldn't be asleep. I walk over to him and shake his shoulder.

"Leave him alone," says Chelsea. "Let's play in the kitchen." She holds up a board game instead of cards.

"I forget how to play," I tell her.

She quick runs through the rules and tells me to get the cards and money in piles.

"You start off with a car and put in a blue piece, since you're a boy." She sticks the plastic pin in for me. "I put in a pink piece since I'm a girl."

Chelsea spins the highest number, so she goes first. She's trying not to smile, but her face is pink, just like her little game piece.

"You kids want another player?" says Dad from behind me. I turn around. He's walking toward us. When he gets to the table, he pulls out a chair and falls into the seat, head drooped against his chest. Chelsea and me don't look at him. We stare straight at each other. Pretend he's not there.

"Go," she says to me louder than before.

I hold my head with one hand and spin with the other.

"Be a winner," says Dad. He's breathing loud through his nose.

Chelsea spins, moves her car. She keeps her attention on the board.

"Who are you talking to?" she asks him. I can barely see her eyes, they're squinted so small.

Dad's looking at the table, not at us.

"That game." He points at the board. His heavy fist drops to the table. "The ads. Says." He holds in a burp. " 'Be a winner.' "

Red blotches cover Chelsea's neck.

"Your turn," she says slow and even.

I can't help but stare at Dad. He keeps jerking his head up, then letting it fall toward his chest again.

"Go!" Chelsea screams at me. She's crying, not even trying to hide it.

All of a sudden Dad gets up and comes over to me, holding on to the table for balance. He bends toward me and whispers in my ear.

"You pick the Farmer card, son?" He's leaning on my shoulder, crushing me with all his weight.

"There is no Farmer card." My heart's banging against my ribs. I want to get away from his huge hands.

"Why not, son?" he asks. "Why isn't there any Farmer card?" He looks confused, like he doesn't know the answer.

" 'Cause you're sure to lose if you pick that card," I say.

Half his mouth breaks into a smile.

"That's my boy," he says. "Good listener." He taps one finger on his head, "Smart," and points at me.

Chelsea pushes her chair away from the table.

"I hate you," she says through her teeth and runs outside.

Dad stumbles back to the couch. I don't know what to do, so I keep playing the game. I pick the Teacher card. According to Chelsea, that's the worst career to have. Since no one's watching, I search through all the cards until I find Doctor.

My game piece leaves Chelsea's in the dust. Boy, is she going to hear it for quitting. I bet she'll punch me. For all I care, she can knock me out cold. When I come to, I'll just stand up and laugh in her face.

I scoot my chair back from the table and head outside.

Poppy's coming toward me on the four-wheeler.

"What do you think, Carter?" He cuts the engine and slides off the back. "Ready to bale hay?"

I show him my muscles and tell him about Mom's ankle weights. He elbows my ribs. Says he'll buy me bigger weights for home.

"Had to sell the herd, you see." His eyes scan the quiet pasture.

"Yeahp," I say and cross my arms.

"Kept your cow, though." He picks up his hat and sets it back on the same spot. "Getting a load of hogs next week. Bud'll help the first couple of days."

Pep's moved away from the green shed to the other side of the pasture.

"Then you don't need my help baling," I tell him.

"We'll see." He presses his blue-and-white handkerchief against his forehead to soak up sweat. When he's finished, he wedges the handkerchief into his back pocket.

"You should sell her." I lean on the fence and kick dirt with my toe. "She won't like being here with the hogs."

He crosses his arms.

"Won't no dairy farmer buy her. Milk's dried up."

Poppy's fixed his attention on me, not the pasture.

"She won't like being here with the hogs," I say again and keep my eyes on his. "Sell her."

He nods once, lets me know he believes I'm a boy with sense.

For a long time, we stand quiet, leaning on the wooden railing.

"Want to ride a bit?" Poppy pats the four-wheeler's seat. "You can drive."

The sun's hot on my neck. I close my eyes and imagine racing through the dirt road's tunnel of trees.

"Maybe after while," I answer. "Not now."

Poppy looks from one end of the pasture to the other.

"Suit yourself." He turns and hurries toward the house.

I know I should call Pep over to me. Whisper in her ear that she was my favorite girl. But I can't. Can't bring myself to say her name.

# How to Hold It All In

WE'RE A cluster of uniformed old boys inside the entryway of the church. We're dressed sharp in navy and smell of aftershave. Not a hair out of place. Our fingernails are clean and our shoes shine. We greet each other, exchange handshakes, gossip. So-and-so's in the hospital, so-and-so's gone to the rest home. It's all the same story, just different names with each telling.

Jinx peers through the doors. "Service is starting."

Used to be we veterans could skip a funeral or two. That was back when there were forty of us or more. Today there's only nine.

We line up two by two and file toward the altar. We sidestep into the pews while Floyd secures the VFW flag in front of the altar stairs. The Stars and Stripes are draped over Chic's casket. The priest swings a burner and leads Chic's family down the aisle. A fog of incense lingers as they pass.

Us old boys look straight ahead, like we're together but in our own separate foxholes. Or coffins. Those who cry are spared the embarrassment of a sideways glance. Those who don't cry sweat at the effort of pushing the emotion down. The heat of it presses against my jacket. I myself don't cry or sweat. I learned long ago how to hold it all in.

We sit. We stand. We do not kneel for fear we won't be able to get back up. We sit again. The priest begins with a reading and then Chic's son Brice takes the podium to deliver the eulogy.

"Dad got his nickname before the ink was dry on his birth certificate. His parents should have just made 'Chic' official since no one ever once called him Francis. The story goes, Dad was born with blonde hair shaded just the slightest bit red. His hair stood up straight off his head like a little chick's."

Brice talks about Chic's love of fishing. How he was always going into detail about some trout or steelhead he caught. Brice tells us how Chic liked to play the lotto.

"He sure was lucky," says Brice, voice catching in his throat. "In numbers and in life."

Even though Brice has developed a paunch and lost most of his hair, I can still see the boy he used to be, with knobby knees too big for his legs and those huge feet and long fingers. He eventually grew into himself, but Chic and me had stopped our Saturday outings years before. I saw Brice every so often uptown at the drugstore buying sugar wafers. He'd say hi and hurry off, keeping his focus on those feet of his. Little did I know how he'd knock our lives off course.

Earlier today we veterans met at the VFW to get ourselves situated for the funeral.

"Didn't think I'd see you here, Marv," Jinx said.

"Why?"

"Well, you know." He opened his hands like a shrug. "Can't remember how many decades it's been since you and Chic spoke."

"I'm here to pay my respects," I said. "Same as everyone else."

I attend the funerals, take part in the ceremonies, but I don't have what you'd call war buddies. And since all the guys my age were in the war, I don't really have buddies. Fine by me. Some guys, all they want to do is talk about the war. Still—to this day! Good God, that's a lot of war talk. Your war stories are your entrance into the gang and I've kept mine all to myself. Even if I start from my first day in the service to my last, I'd've been done finding new stories to add decades ago.

After I said my piece to Jinx, I walked away and found the sign-up sheet. I was writing my name when he came up behind me.

"Marv. Might be best if you present the flag." Jinx liked to run the show.

"Not this time. I'm firing the salute," I said and put the pencil down.

"No need." Jinx picked up the pencil. "We've got it squared."

"Jinx," I said. "I'm firing the salute. Harold can present the flag."

"With that knee of yours and the snow, Marv." He started to erase my name.

"I said I'm firing and I'm *firing*." It was out of character for me, an outburst like that. But I'd had enough. The men averted their eyes and shifted their feet, no doubt shocked. I never challenged Jinx before, even though some say I should be the one doling out orders, if we went by rank.

Chic and me were tight back as schoolboys running the town.

"Follow me," he'd say and I'd try to keep up as we ran in the deep ditches that bordered Highway 18. Sometimes our friend Lyle tagged along. He was a year younger and not as fast.

"You know where the best strawberries are?" asked Chic.

"Sure I do," I said.

Then he stopped. "Where?"

"Why," I said. "The strawberry farm. Claussens."

"Wrong," he said. "Them you have to pay for or steal. And Dad will belt me if I'm caught stealing." He took off and we cut through a cornfield where the sprouts reached just above our ankles. It was early summer, so the corn still had a chance.

We were coming up on the railroad tracks. Lyle trailed behind a couple hundred yards.

"This isn't a trick, is it?" I asked. "I won't play chicken with the train. There's only one winner."

He waved me off. Right next to the tracks he knelt and parted the tall prairie grass. "See here?"

I bent to get a closer look. Sure enough, I saw thin vines and wide leaves and, underneath, small green misshapen nubs covered with seeds. Every so often, we found a red one and popped it in our mouths. They tasted as much like honey as they did strawberries. "You're right. They are the best." I scanned the open fields surrounding us.

Lyle finally caught up. "How'd they get here?"

"They're volunteer," said Chic.

Lyle picked one and ate it. "You threw some tops here?"

"They're from the train. They serve strawberries in the dining car."

"They throw the tops out the window?" I asked.

Then Chic smiled and popped a berry in his mouth. "No. They empty the toilets just before they come into town."

The look on Lyle's face showed enough disgust for the two of us.

Chic was shipped out to France. He was artillery, so he landed in the second wave of D-Day, after the Krauts were cleared from the pillboxes. "What a sight" was all he ever said about it, then his eyes went somewhere else and he shook his head once. I had a lot of "What a sight" moments in the Pacific. I'm sure Chic had others, too. We just never got around to talking about them.

What happened with all us guys who went to war, I believe, was this: as far as home was concerned, we were fighting a valiant war, a war with good cause. But war's war—rot and death and splattered brains and inside-out guts and stink. Because we were the good guys, though, we were meant to keep up the appearance that war was a noble endeavor. And that's where we had a hard time when we came home—tending to the fairy tale.

According to Harriet, on the day we met she saw me first. She was walking uptown with June, Lyle's sister, when she stopped at the photography studio and pointed at my picture. "Now there's a guy I'd like to meet," she said. "Dark-haired and handsome."

To which June replied, "Today's your lucky day, I believe, because he's just across the street." Chic and I were headed to the theater.

"How do you know it's him?" she asked.

"He's friends with my brother Lyle," said June. Then she shouted my name and they hurried to catch us. We all went to watch the film together, then for an ice cream, and Harriet and I saw each other nearly every day after. She was sixteen. I was seventeen. We married the following year, as soon as she graduated high school. Not long after I was shipped across the Pacific to set an island ablaze.

But before that happened we had a few months to ourselves. There's no other word for it than divine. Harriet and I rented a tiny house just beyond the town limits. We were truly in a world of our own. Our nearest neighbor was about a half mile away. Sunday afternoons that summer we'd head down the hill in our backyard toward the creek and hunt blackberries, careful to step around the poison ivy and oak. Harriet was a master picker. She had no trouble avoiding the thorns. All that detail-stitching she'd done sewing clothes trained her hands for patience. Me, I always came home with scratches.

She rinsed the berries in a kitchen towel. We ate them right from the sink till our fingers and lips were stained purple. Afterwards, I'd touch a button on her dress and she'd protest.

"Marvin, you'll stain it." She smiled despite herself.

I touched her lips instead. Then kissed her. Eventually the buttons came undone and we made our way to the bedroom where my inky fingertips teased the cool skin of her stomach.

Just before Chic and I went to war, I asked him, if he came home first, to look in on Harriet. Even though she was moving back in with her parents until it was over, I wanted to hear from him how she was doing. As it turned out, he made it home a full six months before me. The war dragged on in the Pacific and I got badly injured near the end—got my leg chewed up by shrapnel, almost had it amputated, but convinced the doctors to wait. Wait. Wait. They tried a new drug called penicillin, which pushed out the gangrene and saved the leg. I spent a few months in military hospitals before I finally made it home.

All that time I wrote Harriet and heard from her that she had a job as a shop girl uptown selling dresses, but that, as soon as we saved the money, she'd buy her own sewing machine and go into business making clothes and doing alterations and repairs. She told me Chic had taken her and June out for pie one night and that maybe Chic and June might hit it off after all.

On one of the first days I was able to get up and about—slowly, mind you—I found a letter from Chic waiting for me back at my bed. I opened it, surprised to hear from him.

Dear Marv,

I suppose you're enjoying your stay in that hospital bed of yours, being served three squares and cared for by pretty, young nurses and such. Me, I'm already back to work roughing up my hands at the shop. Just tore apart a motor only to discover a mouse had chewed clear through the wires.

I checked in on Harriet like you asked and she's excited to see you. Her spirits are high and she's kept busy at work.

I have to tell you that Lyle was killed in Nice, France.

I didn't want to believe it at first, but Harriet showed me the newspaper clipping and I saw his baby face in a man's uniform and I had to take a seat. I keep expecting him to come home and say it was all a mistake. But he hasn't showed up yet.

June is a lot quieter these days, not as silly as she used to be. June is a different girl.

Take care, old buddy,

Chic

My vision was swimming by the time I finished the letter. I managed to catch the side of the bed before I dropped to the floor, but it didn't help much. My head hit the ground first and all I remember is waking up in bed with a goose egg on my forehead and the urge to scream, to beat my thighs, wail—anything to get the horror out. But no. I wouldn't. I'd take the migraine instead and keep myself held in tight.

Just before I headed home after the war, I wrote Harriet to tell her I was coming in on the train and to meet me at the station. As we rounded the curve just outside of town, the train passed the patch of volunteer strawberries. The ground was covered with snow, but I smiled just the same, then nearly in the same moment, I thought of Lyle and the blood left my face and my fingers started to tingle. I thought for a second I might pass out, so I took a seat on the ground. I'd been standing by the door for the last hour of the trip. My leg was giving me trouble. I stood as soon as the train came to a stop. I wanted to be first one off.

Though it was probably only a few minutes, it felt like a week before the train eased in to the faded red-brick station. I expected to see Harriet and my family—my parents, my sisters. Harriet was there and I lifted her off the ground and would have thrown her in the air like a baby if it hadn't been for my leg. We hugged and kissed and kissed some more. When I finally looked beyond her face, I saw Chic.

We slapped each other's shoulders and said without saying how relieved we were that the other made it home.

"Didn't expect to see you here," I said to him.

"Well, I had use of the car and I thought I'd give you a lift to your parents' house," he said. "Your sisters couldn't all fit and none of them wanted the others to see you first so they stayed home." He laughed.

"Nothing's changed, I see," I said.

Then he made a grimace and the war was back. Everything had changed. Lyle was dead. Other classmates we'd never see again. Friends were missing an arm or both legs. I hadn't heard any details, who else was dead, who was badly hurt, but I knew the news was there waiting for me to take it in.

Chic drove, I sat next to him, then Harriet. They started telling me about who got married, who was going steady, which romances didn't last the war. They were trading stories I hadn't heard and laughing about Don Miller getting caught back of the hardware store with his pants down and Brenda Carey interested in what she saw. Harriet leaned forward to get a good look at Chic and he was beaming at her and I felt an itch in the back of my neck.

"Harriet, how have you been keeping busy?"

Chic said, "Oh, you know she's been working at the shop uptown nearly every day." And he smiled at her and her face turned red.

I stared ahead and said, "I didn't ask you—I asked her."

All the excitement went out of the car. After a few moments of quiet, she spoke, unsure of herself.

"It's like Chic said, I've been working at the shop practically every day, saving for a sewing machine. I help Mom out, making supper and doing chores around the house."

"Have you been going out with June?"

"No," she said. "June's kept to herself since getting the news about Lyle. I've been going to the movies with Marian."

"Anyone else?" I asked.

"Oh, Chic comes with us every once in a while," she said and leaned forward to look at him. "I think he's sweet on Marian."

"She isn't my first choice," he said.

I turned to him. "Who is?"

"I'll tell you when I see her," he said, staring right at Harriet.

When people look at war and study it, it's divided into battles with a clear understanding of who was where, movements, consequences. When we soldiers are in the thick of things, we get our orders and follow them with no knowledge of what's around the next corner. We're in the dark about the big picture.

One battle more than any other has kept me awake over the years. Hill 700 in the Battle of Bougainville. We were just getting ready for breakfast when I got a hurry-up call from Battalion to load up trucks and head for the hills. I was only first looie then. I thought we'd have time to eat so I told my men to get through the mess line pronto. I figured they should get one last hot meal.

To my surprise, the trucks pulled up right away, not in an hour as expected. So much for the hot meal. We moved up the base of the hill, but couldn't use the access road to get to the top. Too dangerous. We'd be sitting ducks. We crawled up the back of Hill 700, which was severely steep and muddy. I felt sorry for the weapon guys—H Co's 81 mm mortars especially, as the tubes weighed 95 pounds and the base plates were a whopping 105 pounds. I had a hard time and I was only carrying a small pack and a carbine.

The next morning at about 8:15 I got a call from second battalion commander who wanted to know how the battle was going. I had to tell him we weren't ready and he said, "Why didn't you get up earlier so we could start on time?" I got irritated and said, "It won't hurt to let the boys live another half hour."

I told the guys to jump off at 8:30. At 8:24 they began throwing the frag grenades. One of the frags came back and hit a guy in the helmet. Lucky for him it didn't go off. After we used up most of the frags, we threw white phosphorus. Those 81 mm mortar smoke rounds were pretty mean.

The Japs figured out my plan and pulled back after we sent the phosphorous bombs their way. That phosphorous, if it touches skin, burns a hole clear through on contact. In fact, it burns a hole through everything but metal. What I should have done was to throw the phosphorous first, then the frags. Imagine having phosphorous rising up around you and then frag grenades bursting all over.

That was the start of the battle for Hill 700 and I lost a lot of men in the fight that followed. Maybe if I'd mixed up the grenades, more men could have made it out alive. But of course, I only understood this after having the benefit of perspective and time to think. Some nights in bed I'd be in the middle of trying to fix a fight, calculate how I could have saved more men or won more ground and Harriet would speak up.

"Marv," she said. "Stop."

"I can't."

"Turn over then." She rubbed the base of my neck and my shoulders until she fell asleep. The heat of her hand through my undershirt and her slow breathing was what eventually calmed me.

We stand at attention on the steps outside the church as a group of young men carry Chic to the hearse. I catch a glimpse of old Jinx trying to keep it together, frowning from the effort. Him and Chic were tight.

The hearse carrying Chic leaves and we break formation.

We walk to the car, quiet with our own thoughts. Cold air stings the tip of my nose. I hitched a ride to the funeral with Floyd and Reggie. My driving isn't what it used to be and I find myself in fear of the ice. Floyd and Reggie take the front and I maneuver myself into the back. What used to be one fluid movement now involves about four or five steps: open the door, hold on to the rail to slide the cane in (though today I'm not using the cane—can't give the boys any ammo for making fun of me), turn to face out, grab onto whatever I can and fall backwards onto the seat, one leg goes in, then the other, scoot a little farther toward the middle, a little farther, take a few deep breaths and look at the wide open door and wonder how the hell I'm going to get it closed.

We're late to the procession of cars, so Floyd drives his own way to make up time, I assume. "Say, where you headed?" I ask him. "The quarry?"

Reggie fixes his cap. "What're you going on about back there?" he asks.

"You're headed the wrong way," I say. "This ain't the way to the cemetery. You're supposed to head south on Main."

Floyd and Reggie exchange a look. "You're all mixed up, Marv," says Reggie. "See the Dairy Twist right there."

I follow where he's pointing. A six-foot plastic ice cream cone sits atop a blue building. The windows are boarded up and the sign in front reads "Closed 4 Wint r."

"The cemetery's no more than a mile thisaway," says Floyd, flicking his right hand toward the windshield. "You forget your glasses?"

"You can see them on top of my nose, can't you?" Why, I think they're right. I am turned around.

"But are you using them?" asks Reggie. Him and Floyd get to laughing up in the front.

I wave them off. "Aahh, who needs you anyway."

"Come on, Marv," says Reggie. "So you got mixed up. It ain't that big a deal."

I watch the fields pass. Almost time to start spring planting. "You think they'll serve a hot meal afterwards or just sandwiches?"

"I expect we'll have fish," says Floyd. He can barely get the words out between laughs. "Seeing as how Chic's being buried in the quarry." And the two of them are back at it, giggling and elbowing each other like a couple of kids at the back of the classroom. Reggie wipes his eyes.

Chic met Eileen at a dance one Saturday night. They married after a couple months of dating and had a son within the year. Harriet still hadn't gotten pregnant. She did her best to appear happy for Chic and Eileen when we paid them and the baby a visit, but once we got home, she went into the bedroom and didn't come out for the rest of the day. I went to the Dairy Twist and bought us hamburgers for supper. Hers sat on the table until the next morning when I threw it out back for the animals to eat.

But life keeps going even when you wish it'd stop—especially when you wish it'd stop—and Chic and Eileen had another boy soon after. Harriet took to the boys and decided she would be an aunt of sorts to them. One Saturday a month, Harriet and Eileen had card club so Chic and I brought the boys to the quarry in the summer, sledding in the winter. At the quarry, we sat on a blanket in the shade drinking beer while the boys played. One summer day, little Brice came up to me and gave my arm a hug and Chic saw that it made me happy and sad all at once.

"Do you and Harriet plan to adopt?"

I sat up and stared at the water and said, "We've never discussed it." The sunlight sparkled on the ripples and I had to look away. "We never discuss anything about children. It's like a bubble of silence between us that grows bigger every day."

"Then I suppose it's time you brought it up," said Chic.

Harriet wouldn't hear anything about adoption.

"I won't do it," she said. "I'm going to have one of my own. I want to feel a baby moving inside me. We just have to keep trying."

"It's been four years."

She was at the sink washing dishes facing the window. She spoke over her shoulder, "Then what's four more? I'm not barren yet."

After the war, I found work as a bricklayer. On rare occasion, the work took me out of town on a job. When that happened, I called over to Chic's and asked would he stop in and check on Harriet, to which he said, "Sure, Marv." I never told Harriet I'd sent Chic her way. Her seamstress work had grown to where she'd begun to talk about hiring a girl. If I'd said I was having Chic stop in and see she was okay, she would have told me I was being silly, that she could take care of herself.

On one such job, we finished a day earlier than expected and I drove the five hours home after working a full day. By the time I got home it was pitch black, closing in on nine o'clock. It was November and night came earlier every day. I walked into the quiet house and didn't find Harriet in the kitchen or front room so I walked back to our bedroom and stopped in my tracks when Chic stepped out of the bathroom buttoning his pants.

"Where's Harriet?" I asked.

He was surprised to see me. "She's—she's in the bedroom."

I stared him in the eyes for a moment and opened the bedroom door. Harriet was in her underwear about to put on a dress.

"What the hell is going on?"

She yelped, clutched the dress to the front of her. "Marv. You scared me."

"Did I? I guess you were expecting someone else."

"I wasn't expecting anyone. I was getting dressed."

"The question is why?"

"I was trying on a dress I thought Chic might want me to make for Eileen for Christmas."

I went out to the hall. Chic stood there with his eyes wide.

"Am I to believe you came over here to look at a dress?"

He put his hands up to stop me. "No. You told me to come check in on her. That's why I was here."

"That doesn't explain why she's in her underwear."

"She was showing me a dress for Eileen. She's telling the truth."

Harriet was dressed by then and came out to the hall. "He stopped in and I told him I was cold, that the heater wasn't working. He said the pilot light was out, he lit it, and we talked about winter coming on, then Christmas."

I stared at the two of them, searching for a clue to the truth.

Floyd drives us to the section of the cemetery where everyone's spilling out of their cars. Even though there's snow on the ground, the sky is blue as a Pacific lagoon, the clouds are few and far between and the sun is shining. Perfect day to handle steel.

Once we're outside, Jinx passes me a rifle. I check it's loaded and ready to go. The crowd watches as the men bring the casket to the grave site.

"Line up," says Jinx.

Floyd moves to the front, then Reggie, then a few other guys. I bring up the rear. We wait as the priest begins the prayer. The wind freezes my fingers. My toes are numb.

The sergeant at arms gives the commands. He's a young guy—served in Iraq.

I have a hard time lifting my legs to a full march. I scuff my feet across the pavement. At the lip onto the snow-covered grass, Floyd falters. The ice-covered snow crunches with each step. I give it my all and march as hard as I can. I stomp onto the snow and slip a notch forward. I focus on the grave marker and count down the distance: twenty feet, fifteen. We stop at ten. I'm clear out of breath. My lungs feel like they're ready to split.

Harriet went into labor in mid-July, a month before her due date. I sat out in the sweltering waiting room and smoked till my throat hurt. I wasn't a smoker in the first place, but the two other men waiting with me kept offering and I never refused.

The nurse finally came out with the news: I was the father of a little girl and was I ready to see her?

"Is she healthy?" I asked.

She led me to the nursery. "Very," she said.

"Even though she's a month premature?"

"Is she?" said the nurse, surprised. "She's near six pounds. It might be good luck your wife had her early. She could have been an eight-pound baby if she'd gone full term."

She brought me to the window and pointed her out to me. I couldn't find her at first.

"Right there," said the nurse. "First row, second from the left."

I finally found her. If the nurse hadn't been there, I would have cried, but I held it in and breathed and breathed and had to sit down.

"We were going to put a cap on her," said the nurse, who bent down to speak to me. She was smiling. "But we wanted you to see her beautiful hair first."

The hair was blonde with the slightest bit of red. It stood up straight off her head like a little chick's and I did the calculation and I knew.

Oh, she denied it, of course. Chic, too.

"My aunt has red hair," said Harriet, hysterical, pacing the kitchen with the baby in her arms, feeding her a bottle.

"Do you see my hair?" I said. "It's black. Dark eyes. I got Indian in me." I moved to the far end of the kitchen, as far from her as I could get. "That child is not mine."

"She is!" she screamed. The baby choked on her milk and shrieked in her little bird voice until Harriet sat down at the table with her and I left.

The decision to stay or leave for good was made harder by the fact that I couldn't talk to Lyle—the only person I would have turned to for advice. Such decisions, however, aren't made at the end of a long session alone with one final drop of the gavel. They happen a little at a time. I stayed at my parents' house, claiming Harriet and I were having a hard time adjusting to the baby and she needed time to herself. I went back to our house, though, to get a change of clothes and give her some money—I wasn't going to let them starve—and the baby was asleep in her arms and I couldn't help myself. I sat down.

"If you just held her—" said Harriet, easing her into my arms.

"No," I said, even though I was already holding her. She poked her hand out of the blanket and grabbed my finger and sighed and I stayed longer than I'd intended. Then I came back the next day, just to check on them, mind you, and ate the lunch Harriet fixed for me. Then dinner the next day and the night after I stayed so late I had to sleep there. Then I stayed for good.

Chic and I never spoke again. Eventually up at the VFW the guys wanted to know what the hell was the matter anyway. I made up a story about how I lent Chic my lawn mower and he claimed I gave it to him. And Floyd or Jinx or some other guy would say, "Aach, you two need to just get over it. Busting up a friendship over a lawn mower?" and he'd wave me off. But they believed it and they liked having something to talk about. Chic never disputed the story, even did his part to keep up the ruse, adding in his own details that made their way back to me, how he'd offered me ten dollars and I refused. He told the boys, "Sometimes a bunch of little things add up to one big break." At least that much was true.

We make it to our spot in the snow and stop our march. I'm relieved just to be in place and not moving in any one direction. My fingers don't work like they used to. Sometimes I'll bend my ring finger and it won't come back up on its own. I have to unlock it and push it back straight.

"Firing squad do your duty," says Jinx.

"Present arms," says the kid.

I lift my gun and hold myself steady.

"Fire!"

I'm worried I'll be late for the next volley. I'd rather miss the shot entirely than come in late.

But when the kid yells "Fire!" I do.

None of us told Eileen. Harriet and Eileen tried to keep up their friendship, but it was too much to overcome, the men no longer friends. Eileen even said to me once, "You know, we can give it back, Marv. It's just a lawn mower." And I felt terrible, lying to her in more ways than one, like I was just as guilty as Chic and Harriet for what they'd done. But once you start a lie, you have to prune it and water it, pull the weeds—like a garden. After that, though, I told Harriet I couldn't be around Eileen and that was the end of their friendship.

As for Rose, after I held her that first time, I couldn't help myself. I was hers. Whatever she wanted (within reason, mind you)—she knew who to ask.

Rose was a good girl, eager to please us but also enjoyed the benefits of being an only child. Her trouble started when she entered high school. She got mixed up with the wrong crowd. It was the cars that did it. Once a child starts going around in cars, she has a false sense of freedom. Like she can go anywhere and do anything because she steps inside a different world and the leather seat transports her to a place with no rules. There she went, night after night, believing she was invincible. Until she wasn't. A friend drove off the road into the ditch and banged up everyone inside. Rose was lucky to make it out with a black eye. Harriet and I thought that would be the end of it, but trouble followed her home.

One night I heard a noise out back and thought a raccoon might have gotten into the trash cans. I went around the side of the house with a flashlight and came upon Rose with a boy. I shined the light on him and saw it was Chic's son, Brice.

"You get out of here," I yelled at him. "And you"—I pointed at Rose—"go inside."

Brice hurried away and I went in to Rose's bedroom, where she was crying, embarrassed and angry.

"You stay away from that boy," I said to her. "He's no good."

"You're wrong." And then, near a shout, she said, "He's my friend."

"I'm no dummy," I said. "Boys and girls aren't friends." I grabbed the top of her arm so she'd face me. "You're to stay away from him."

She just stared at me, wiping tears.

"Understand?"

"Leave me alone!" she screamed.

And I slapped her. The one and only time.

Of course, some things in life you can only learn by experience. That which you forbid a teenager becomes the teenager's sole focus. A few months later I walked into the kitchen, where Rose was in tears and Harriet stood at the sink holding her temples, breathing uneasy.

"What?" I said.

Both looked at me, then each other, but neither would speak.

"What?" I grew impatient. "Out with it."

"She's in a bad way," said Harriet in a shaky voice.

"Surely you don't mean—"

"She's pregnant," said Harriet finally.

With those words, the truth I'd distanced myself from over time, that Rose wasn't truly my daughter, uppercut my chin. I couldn't believe my own lie anymore.

"My God," I said. "They're brother and sister!"

"What?" said Rose, confused.

"No, they are not!" screamed Harriet.

"What's he talking about?" asked Rose.

"Tell her, Harriet," I said. "Tell her about Chic."

"There's nothing to tell," said Harriet. "Just a story in your head."

"What about Chic? Are you saying you're not my dad?" asked Rose.

"I raised you, didn't I? Then I'm your dad."

"Then what's going on?"

"He thinks I had an affair with Chic," said Harriet. "I didn't."

"You know what? You two figure out your own crap right now. I have enough to deal with." She left the kitchen and slammed the door.

Once Rose couldn't hide anymore under big sweaters and dresses, we found a place run by nuns in southern Ohio that took in girls in her situation. I drove Rose there and carried her suitcase up a flight of stairs and set it on a narrow bed. The other bed in the room was made and a few personal items—a comb, a toothbrush—were on a shelf next to it. I hugged Rose and told her I'd see her in a few months when this mess was over and done with. It seemed like I was simply dropping her off at camp, which is what we told everyone in town since she'd be there for the summer.

Harriet visited her twice, bringing her cookies and home-made bread and Coke. Then one evening we got a phone call at home from Rose telling us she was about to have the baby. Harriet packed an overnight bag and changed into her good clothes.

"Where are you going?"

"To be with her," she said.

"At this time of day? It isn't safe," I said.

"I'm a careful driver."

"You might get attached to the baby and want to keep it," I said.

"And so what if I do?"

"I'm not raising another child." We both knew what I meant. I wasn't raising another child that wasn't mine.

"I'll be back tomorrow," she said and left.

I was nervous and couldn't focus. I went to work and hardly did a thing. I started a task—laid out the base for a chimney—and got distracted and an hour later, I'd be starting at the same run of bricks and realize I hadn't made a single move.

When Harriet returned, she came in the kitchen with an air of confidence, like she'd just won a contest. Smug even.

"Is there a baby in the car?" I asked.

"No," she said.

"Boy or girl?"

"Boy."

"Has he been adopted?" I asked.

"He has." She put on her apron and opened the refrigerator door.

"Is he—healthy?"

"Perfectly healthy." She closed the fridge, put two onions on the counter and cut one in half. "I took a picture of him. It's at the drugstore now, being developed." She wiped her eyes with the back of her wrist and kept chopping.

"The drugstore? You know how that Chambers gossips. What will you tell him about the baby?"

"I already told him," she said. "It was a friend's son's baby." She dropped the onions in a bowl, then a packet of meat. "Which isn't a lie really."

"I don't want to see any picture," I said. "I want no part of it."

She broke an egg and crushed some crackers and mixed up a meatloaf. The next night at dinner she put the picture on my plate before serving the leftovers. I couldn't look away and, even worse, found my nose moving closer to it.

I saw Rose first and knew from the photograph she was in shock. Her face was blank and her eyes were dull. Then I looked at the boy. He had hair black as an Indian's and dark eyes. What I couldn't get over, though, was his cleft chin. Just like mine.

Rose wasn't the same after she came home, like the baby had pulled all the happiness out of her with him. She didn't brush her long, soft hair. It turned stringy and knotted, and she often lost her place in her thoughts. We tried to cheer her up, bought her the horse she'd always wanted and it helped some. The horse required care and she needed to care for something.

My relationship with Harriet changed, too. She was calmer now, vindicated. Less meek. She spoke up for herself more and I found myself growing quieter. So much had happened between Chic and me that, even though I knew I'd been wrong, we couldn't speak to each other anymore. It would feel unnatural to talk to him, like neither of us had used our own voice in so long that it might not make a sound if we tried.

Want to know how to hold it all in? Hurt yourself. Pinch your skin right above the wrist until you're certain it'll bruise. Bite the inside of your cheeks until they bleed. When you're in a spot where guys are looking at you for guidance, pleading with their eyes, "Promise me it'll be okay," and you've got the blood of one of your boys splattered across your face, you goddamn well lie. "Fire!"

Harriet died on a Sunday a few months after we celebrated our sixty-eighth wedding anniversary. I found her in her pink rocking chair with her knitting needles limp in her fingers. Her mouth had gone slack, her gray eyes focused on the pine trees beyond the picture window.

I didn't cry, but I found I couldn't muster the strength to make funeral arrangements. Even buttering toast in the morning felt like an enormous task. Opening the fridge to get the butter took all my energy. The knife weighed more than I could lift. So Rose did it all—made the funeral arrangements, called the relatives with the viewing schedule, planned the meal afterward, brought me to the funeral home and back, loaded the flowers in the car after it was all over.

Rose never married. It broke Harriet's heart, that she never had any grandchildren. She also worried about Rose as she grew older. She would be completely alone. Rose didn't mind a bit, though. She said she preferred it actually. She'd taught kindergarten and claimed she'd spent most of her life surrounded by children. She loved how quiet her life had become.

On the last evening of Harriet's viewing, at the end of the night after the visitors had all gone, Rose checked the clock and said she supposed we could leave. She helped me get my coat on when the door opened and in walked Chic and Brice.

A couple months after Rose gave up the boy for adoption and the sadness was still stuck to her, I took her out for a hamburger.

A few bites in, I asked, "Have you seen Brice?"

She kept chewing, picked up a fry, ate that then finally said, "Here and there."

"Might do you some good to talk to him," I said.

The blood rose in her cheeks. "Now you want me to talk to him? You said he was no good."

"Well, he did end up being trouble, didn't he?"

Then she grew quiet.

"He's the only one you can talk to about all this. The only one who knows."

She looked out the window. "I can't—he's going steady with another girl."

And now here he was, practically a stranger, with Chic staring at us in the funeral home.

"Hi, guys," said Rose and she went up to them and hugged them both. "Mom's back here." And she led them to the casket while I stood there like a dummy. Brice nodded as he passed. The three of them faced her and talked in quiet voices, then all of a sudden, Chic started to sob.

"What a loss," he said. "What a loss."

I had to leave. His crying felt like a sickness I might catch if I stayed too near. And if I cried, I might crack open and never get back together. I went to the restroom and took my time. When I went back out front, Chic and Brice were gone and Rose was dabbing her eyes with a folded tissue.

I'm on the ground trying to fill my lungs, making dramatic sounds, but I cannot get enough air in. I'm staring up at sky and the sting of the frigid snow is pressing against my back. As hard as I try to stop them, the sobs form in my lungs, tumble past my ribs and out of me. I can feel the focused stare of every person here, which is torture, but also a relief. The buildup to facing fear is always worse than the fear itself.

Everyone's standing above me or trying to help me up and I just want to stay on the ground for a moment, cold as it is, and catch my breath.

"Are you okay, Marv?" asks Reggie. "Can you get up?"

If everyone would just go away, I'd take my time and get up at my own pace. I finally notice a woman kneeling next to me. I study her for a moment and realize it's June.

"Come on, Marv," she says. "Let me help you up." She offers me a hand. I take it and can feel the warmth through the glove. With her other hand, she pushes me up by the shoulders. "Is your hip okay? Do you think you can walk?"

"Yes, yes," I say. "I'm fine, everyone. Just my pride that's bruised. Thank you for your concern." She winds her arm around mine and walks me to the passenger side of her car. It feels strange to have a woman guiding me to a door, rather than the other way around.

I sit down and she starts the car. Everyone else is leaving and she lets them go first. Floyd comes to the window.

"June, you can give him a ride home?"

" 'Course I can." She lets the cars go and we're the only mourners left. "Do you want to get a coffee?" she asks. "I could bring you straight home, if not. But I just figured, I'm going back to an empty house and so are you—"

Rose moved up to Michigan years ago, right after she graduated college. She's been pushing me to sell the house and move in with her, to which I respond, why not sell her house and move in with me? It's the house she grew up in, after all. But she's so involved in her church, she can't leave. They're like a family to her. She has no friends in New Marburg anymore. It'd be like starting over at sixty and she just can't.

"Yes," I say. "It sure is empty." And I look at all the gravestones. Harriet's isn't far away and my name's already carved next to hers. Only thing missing is the date of my death. "Seems like, we all start as a complete puzzle. Parents, sisters and brothers, friends. As the years go on, pieces of the puzzle go missing never to be found again."

She nods.

"You get new pieces, of course. Like children."

"And grandchildren." She blushes, believes she's made a mistake. She takes off her gloves and puts them on the seat between us. "I'm sorry you never had any."

And suddenly I don't have it in me anymore, the strength to tell one more lie. "I did have one. A boy."

She studies my face. "I do remember some talk about Rose, how she might have been in trouble, but it's been so long, I'd forgotten."

"We told everyone Rose went to summer camp, but she was at a home run by the nuns." I feel tired, like I could take a nap right now, right here. "Harriet made it just in time to see him being born." And then, June's wiping tears and I don't know how it happens, but I'm crying and then the sobs are shaking clear through me and June's crying, too. All I can manage to say is "Harriet" and I grab June's forearm with my hand and she holds onto mine and there we sit wiping tears, holding arms.

"Harriet was a class act," she says finally. "Sure, we drifted apart, but—" She shrugs. "When I think back on our friendship, it's as if our time as friends lasted just as long as it was supposed to."

"I miss her," I say, then: "We didn't get enough time with Lyle." I regret it as soon as I speak. I don't think she's ever gotten over his death, that she's carried it with her through life like a key that stays on her keychain even though she can't remember which lock it opens.

"Maybe you're looking at it the wrong way," she says. "Maybe our time with him was the gift, rather than the time without him the punishment." She pulls tissues from her coat pocket and offers me one.

I take it. We wipe our cheeks and pinch our noses clean.

"Lyle could be a son of a gun when he wanted to," she says. "He wasn't always nice."

"None of us are."

She pushes her used tissue up the sleeve of her coat, ready in case she needs it again. "Every once in a while, I'd turn the corner in our house and get whapped in the face with a heavy feather pillow," she says. "It knocked me to the ground. Next thing I knew Lyle was beside me, laughing too hard to stand. He was ornery."

I tell her about Lyle and Chic and me eating the strawberries. How, after Chic said they came from the toilets, Lyle spit and spit and swatted at his tongue. We get to laughing like we're kids again. The windows are fogging up and I bet if anyone came upon the car, they'd think something steamy was going on. And you know what I say?

Let 'em.

# Just Les Is Fine

I WAS dead set against having an anniversary party for Joan and me, but Carla pushed for it. Every excuse I came up with—it'd be too much work, too much planning, too much money, too much, too much, too much—Carla knocked down.

"You and Mom need to celebrate," she said. "Twenty-five years is a big deal."

The Sunday before the party, I opened the office for Carla's friend Naomi. She and Carla were both in town for their classmate's wedding and Carla had asked me to check Naomi's eyes as a favor. I told her of course I would, even though I hadn't seen Naomi as a patient in years.

I unlocked the front door and waited in my office. I caught up on paperwork and fooled around with the computer. Some Saturdays I made an excuse to be in the office alone. Even then, in 2003, I'd found the porn. Or rather, it had found me.

"Hi, Doc Miller." Naomi's hips rocked with each step. High-heel sandals, tight white shorts. Hair the color of split redwood.

I pictured her hips, naked and searching for mine. I pinched my thigh so hard my eyes watered. If I could have punched myself, I would have. She was my daughter's friend. Hardly older than the teenager who ate lunch in my kitchen, legs pretzeled around her chair, sucking cheese powder off her fingertips.

"Naomi," I said, voice breaking. I coughed a clear space in my throat. "Sit down. Please." I motioned to the chair across from me. Standing was out of the question. "You don't have to call me Dr. Miller. Just Les is fine."

She came to my side of the desk and bent to hug me. All I could see was the bunch of her breasts. Best I could offer was a sideways hug.

"Rude of me not to stand," I said, shrugging helplessly. "Back's been giving me problems all week."

Naomi wrinkled her forehead. "Are you okay?"

"Nothing serious." I fumbled with my bifocals, dropped them on the desk. I smoothed the hair just above the back of my neck, the beard around the corners of my mouth.

"Well," I said. *Well, what?* "You're a woman now."

Her face blossomed pink, then red. She stared at her lap, pressed her lips into a smile.

"I guess I am." She raised her eyes, pale as green grapes on the vine.

"So." Hard as I tried, I couldn't stop the idiotic slow nod that had taken over my head.

"So." She looked behind me at the framed diplomas on the wall. "I like that your office is in an old Victorian. It gives the place character."

"Buying the Victorian was Joan's idea."

"She decorated it, then?"

"Oh no, my office manager, Lynn, did," I said. "If she could have things her way, this place would be all pink and lace and stuffed with dolls."

Naomi laughed. "So you managed to talk her down to the antiques?"

"It wasn't easy." I stood—finally—and motioned for her to follow me to the exam room. "How have you been?"

"Decent," she said.

I opened the door and turned on the lights.

She sat in the chair. "And you?"

"Good," I said. "Really good."

I positioned the phoropter in front of her. "We're going to get a measure of your prescription first." I went through the lenses on both eyes.

"Good thing you came in. Your prescription needs adjustment." I moved the phoropter away from her and she gave me a smile. I had to turn my back to her and busy myself with scribbling on the prescription pad. I struggled to steady my hand.

I picked up the retina scope. "Let's get a good look in there." I leaned in close to her, one leg between hers. My heart thumped in my ears. The leg between hers brushed against her knee.

Naomi told me she was thinking about changing careers—accounting bored her—and could she shadow me one day? I laughed and told her optometry wasn't the most exciting field either, but, of course, she could.

"When?"

I should have put her off for a while, said it was a busy time of year, the month before school started, which was the truth. But I craved the sight of her.

"I'm open Saturdays now and closed on Mondays. Does next Saturday work? You're coming to the anniversary party, aren't you?" I put the retina scope down and scribbled.

She looked confused. "Whose anniversary party?"

"Ours," I said, puzzled. "Didn't Carla invite you?" I stood and turned up the lights in the exam room.

She shook her head no.

We walked out to the hallway. "Well, I'm inviting you right now."

"I don't know if I can come. My boyfriend's coaching his baseball team in the playoffs next weekend."

I gave her the prescription then we stood awkwardly in the waiting room saying our goodbyes.

"How much do I owe you?" she asked.

"I wouldn't think of charging you," I said. "My pleasure."

"No," she said, digging in her purse. "It's not right. I have to pay you something."

I held up a hand. "I know what you can do."

She stopped searching her purse and waited.

"Come to the party."

Her shoulders relaxed. "Okay," she said. "It'll be nice to see Carla again. And—next Saturday? I can shadow you?"

"Yes!" I said. Then, trying to be clever: "It's a date."

She gave me a confused smile. "Sure."

[**Character Study**[1]

## Who Is Les?
*Every other Monday, Les volunteers on the children's floor at the local hospital. Mostly he holds sick babies whose parents can't be at the hospital all hours because they're working or have other kids. Of course, there are bad parents, too, but he tries to forget about them. Les regrets not holding Carla more when she was a baby. He was*

---

1    All text in brackets belongs to the **Character Study**.

*busy getting the office up and running and didn't realize how quickly she'd move from sleeping in his arms to crawling.*

*Les has always done the right thing in life and now he finds it frustrating, constantly following the rules. He wants to have fun, live a little. He became an optometrist because he could be a doctor, yet work office hours—no holidays, weekends, or on-call. He has always liked the repetition, the predictability of his job. But now it's wearing on him.*

*His parents didn't talk to each other much. His father worked as an insurance man, his mother kept herself busy, constantly busy, with volunteering at the school, the church, the Ladies Auxiliary— anything that kept her out of the house, which she liked to remind her kids was her "gilded cage." His older sister has been in and out of mental hospitals her whole adult life. He knows he will be responsible for her well-being in the near future, as well as his parents' when they can no longer live on their own.*

*He feels like the caretaking stage is almost upon him and his last chance for freedom is slipping away. He wants to feel strong—a guy people give a respectful distance to.*]

The night before the party, I still hadn't figured out an anniversary gift. My first idea went bust and I was in a bind. I thought about what Joan liked to do, which was run. Every day Joan ran, as if her destination were forever around the next corner.

So I decided to buy her a new CD Walkman and headphones. But when I got to Radio Shack, the sales guy showed me this device called an iPod—back in 2003 it really was a sight to behold—and I thought, *Perfect. Two birds, one stone.* Her music wouldn't skip or weigh her down while she ran and I could use the iPod at home instead of our portable CD player.

I had to get rid of that CD player. It knew too much.

[Who is Joan?

*Joan was the favored daughter in her family, but she also had the responsibilities of caring for her younger siblings. She wanted to go to college to become a teacher, but her mother always told her she was the pretty one, not the smart one—she shouldn't put too much stake in college.*

*Joan had a need to achieve and, as a senior in high school, was crowned queen of the county fair. Les saw Joan take the title just after he graduated from Ohio State. He managed to meet her after the ceremonial crowning and made her laugh by asking her if winning meant she got the key to the pig stalls. He liked that she had laughed and she liked that he had made her laugh instead of treating her like a flower whose petals were about to fall off. They married three years later and had Carla a year after that. They tried to have more children, but Joan miscarried twice and they never had another child.*

*Joan pushed Carla to go to college, encouraged her to study and be smart. When Carla left for college, Joan felt lost. She didn't know what to do to fill her time, so she began fixing up the house. First, she ripped down wallpaper, then the carpet. She was cleaning out gutters before having the exterior painted when she fell and broke her back. "Through the grace of God," her spine was saved, but she cracked two vertebrae. After the fall, she was in the hospital, then physical therapy for months. All work on the house stopped. Eventually Joan began to walk. Then run. She runs marathons now and could be described as skeletal.*]

In the summers when Carla was in elementary school, we spent every weekend camping. Joan and I figured we'd only get a few more years of her attention, so we bought an RV and off we went. Carla made friends quickly and soon she was running around the campground with a pack of dirty-soled kids.

Joan never much liked camping. "Why drive clear across the

state when I still have to cook and clean? It's not really a vacation for me, especially since I have an extra load of laundry to do when we get home."

"Lighten up, Joan," I said, "You don't think this is extra work for me, too? That I camp so I can set up a sewage line? It isn't about us. Look at Carla." She was counting kids, dividing them into teams. "She loves it."

That was back when Joan and I could have arguments. It was back when we had sex, too. Carla talked in her sleep, so we waited until we heard her mumbling, then hid under the covers and held in our laughs.

"What if she hears us?" asked Joan.

"We'll tell her we were wrestling." I sucked on her earlobe. She loved it, even though she always pulled back, saying it tickled.

[Who is Carla?

*As a girl, Carla did everything she could to please her mother. She was an overachiever in school and did all the activities her mother had done—or wished she'd done: cheerleader, ballerina, then marching band field commander. She was accepted to every college she applied to and chose Oberlin.*

*Carla's rebellion in college was to continue to achieve, but in a major neither of her parents understood: Women's Studies. She became a Buddhist and stopped going to church, much to the distress of her parents. Carla didn't become the lawyer her mother wanted and instead chose to work for little money at a nonprofit environmental organization in Cleveland. For a summer during college, she followed Phish around, making grilled-cheese sandwiches by wrapping them in tin foil and ironing them in exchange for pot. At the end of the summer, she went back to work to pay for a much-needed abortion.*

Les-Joan-Carla dynamic

*Joan still has hope Carla's just going through a phase and she'll come around and get back to being who Joan wanted her to be. Les is less optimistic. He hopes she'll change her appearance—get rid of those god-awful dreadlocks and lose just ten, but, let's be serious, forty pounds of the extra weight she's put on. He doesn't say much anymore about her career. As long as she goes to church when she's home, she can do what she wants when she's back in Cleveland. Carla spends less and less time with her parents these days. Eighteen years solid with the same two people was plenty for her.*

*Joan goes to bed early and sleeps in late, essentially spending very little time with Les. She leaves to run just as he's pulling in the drive, even in the winter. She returns from her run, eats what he's left in the oven, showers, sits in front of the TV or goes to the computer—whichever is the opposite of what Les is doing—and goes to bed.*]

I made sure to get my hair cut the day before Naomi shadowed me. Even had Mel trim up my beard. I bought a new outfit at the mall. "Something young," I told the sales gal. She put me in a pair of flat-front black pants and a bright blue golf shirt.

"Don't you look sharp," said Naomi as she greeted me with a hug. There she was again, looking like a Wyeth painting come to life. But with high heels, a miniskirt, tanned legs.

Lynn held the door open and stood staring at us. "It's going to be a busy day, Les," she said as she handed me the patient list across my desk.

I scanned the list. "I'm double-booked all over the place. What's so urgent about Ethel Turnbald's cataracts?"

Lynn left my office, pulling the door with her. "You know Ethel. Everything's urgent."

I knew she'd done it on purpose, double-booking me. Just to let me know she didn't like Naomi being there.

"Well, then," I said. "You want to be an optometrist."

She wrapped her folded hands around her knee, arched her back. "That's what I'm here to find out."

When we finished the morning's exams, I asked Naomi about lunch. Usually I ate at my desk—tomato soup or tuna on saltine crackers. "Would you like to go out to eat?"

She thought for a moment. "The Filling Station?" It was an old gas station converted into a pizza place.

That would take at least an hour. Lynn only slotted me a half hour for lunch. I'd smell like smoke for the rest of the afternoon.

"Sounds good."

Our waitress was the town gossip, Diane Miller. She lifted an eyebrow at Naomi and me and I told her what we were doing there, just the two of us: "Naomi is thinking about becoming an optometrist."

"Is that so?" said Diane, putting her order book on her round tray. Naomi nodded.

"She's spending the day in our office."

"Umm hmm," said Diane.

When our pizza came, I held my slice above my plate and let the orange grease pond in the center. "Tell me again why you're thinking about marrying this guy if you aren't sure."

"I want to go back to school," she said. "He'll help out with that. Plus I've been paying part of the mortgage on his house. It'll be a big mess if I leave."

I patted more grease from the slick cheese with a crumpled napkin. "Sometimes the only way to set things right is to make a mess."

She shimmied a piece of the pizza free from the disc with the spatula.

"Marriage is hard enough," I said. "Make sure it's really what you want before you commit."

"What's so hard about it?"

I wanted to say compromise. I planned on saying compromise. "It's lonely."

She drank a sip of beer. I followed and took such a mouthful that it filled my throat, stinging as it went down.

"I don't understand," she said. "Isn't it the opposite?" She wiped her mouth with a napkin. "That's what scares me. Constantly being with the same person, day after day."

I ate the front corner of my pizza. "At first you can't stand to be away from each other. Then you start to argue about things, like if she cooks, shouldn't you do the dishes. Then a baby comes along and, at some point, you each pick your corner and stay there. The only time you meet in the middle is for a fight."

Naomi stared at me, mouth half open. "Maybe it's a matter of choosing the right person," she said. "It can't be the same for everyone."

Somewhere I'd veered off course. We'd started lunch laughing about Ethel. I wanted to keep her smiling and laughing, but we'd taken a serious turn that I couldn't steer out of.

"First it was just the pain after Joan's accident. At least I felt like I could help her with that. But now—" I looked around to make sure no one was listening. "I can't remember the last time we had a conversation."

When Joan fell from the ladder, she was clearing leaves from the gutter. I'd told her that I would do it the following weekend, but she couldn't wait. Even though I had nothing to do with her fall, I knew she blamed me, as if I had made her climb the ladder, then pushed her off.

"I'm sure Joan will come around, Les." She clasped a hand over mine.

Goosebumps traveled up my arm. I told her about how hard these past years had been. "It's not much of a life."

"For her or for you?" Naomi asked.

My face felt hot with sudden embarrassment. I'd told her too much.

"Do you ever fantasize about running away?" I asked. "You know, just starting a whole new life?" My heart thumped my ribs. I'd gone too far.

She looked up. "Sometimes."

[Who is Naomi?

*Naomi was a sickly child. Every winter, she caught whatever flu was going around. Her mother tried for a while to give her the attention she craved, but she grew numb to Naomi's constant needs. Her father moved to Virginia years ago and she rarely sees him. Naomi's mother worked most evenings as the manager of a drugstore in town. When she was younger, Naomi spent a lot of time at friends' houses to avoid being home alone. At one point, Carla's house was one she made daily treks to. She usually did this for a year, then the family either got sick of her or she moved on to another friend. Ninth, tenth, eleventh, twelfth grades—she had a different best friend for each year of school. She was in tenth grade when she spent all her time at Carla's.*

*Naomi likes attention as long as it's on her terms. Too much drives her away. As for the attention she gives, she doesn't like expectations. She met her current boyfriend in college. He's a gym teacher, with baseball as his preferred sport. She hates baseball, finds it infinitely boring.*]

After lunch with Naomi, I called Lynn and told her I was sick, to cancel all my appointments.

"What's wrong?" I heard the shock in her voice. Never in all my years had I canceled an afternoon of appointments.

"Food poisoning, I think." I stared at Naomi sitting alone at the table. Then I lowered my voice. "I've already been to the bathroom twice."

"Oh," said Lynn.

I went back to the table and said, "Come on. Let's play hooky."

Naomi looked up at me. "What do you mean? Don't we have to get back?"

"I have to buy Joan a gift and I could use your help."

"Okay," she said. "What kind of gift?"

"A piece of jewelry," I said. "What do you think?"

She lifted a shoulder. "I think she'd expect that." She stood and we went toward the door.

"You know," I reached the door first and held it open for her, "she could use a new car."

She stopped and turned. "Now *that's* unexpected."

We went to Boyd's, the only car dealer in town. Boyd himself came out when he saw us strolling between cars.

"Doc," he said, shaking my hand. Then he turned to Naomi, scanned her up and down. "Carla? Wow, you've grown up."

Naomi smiled, gave me a nervous look. "I'm actually Naomi, Carla's friend."

"Ope," said Boyd. "Sorry about that." He studied me for an explanation and got none. "What can I do you for?"

The heat rose off the blacktop. The air was so thick I felt like I couldn't fully catch my breath.

"Tomorrow's my anniversary," I said. "I'm thinking about buying Joan a car."

Boyd clasped his hands together and rubbed his palms. "I'd say you're in the right place." He smiled. "What kind of car are we talking about?"

Naomi lifted her hair off her neck and fanned it.

I stared. I imagined how soft her skin was, like a newly picked nectarine. "A convertible."

"That narrows things down then," said Boyd. "We only have two." He led us to a pair of Sebrings. One red, one silver.

"Which one?" I asked Naomi.

"Well, it's your silver anniversary," she said. "So—red." She threw her head back and laughed and there was her neck again. Boyd and I were in a trance. If she'd've told us to stand in the middle of oncoming traffic, we'd have asked, "Northbound or southbound?"

"I'm going to need a test drive," I told Boyd.

"Sure thing, Doc."

While he went in to get the keys, I opened the passenger door for Naomi. She slid into the leather seat and ran a hand across the glove compartment. Boyd passed me the keys and asked me not to take it over sixty.

"Wouldn't think of it," I said.

Boyd came over to my side of the car to explain how to get the top down, but I stopped him. "Already have it figured, Boyd. See you in a few."

He backed away and I put the car in drive and floored it. I saw the shock on his face in the rearview mirror and laughed. Naomi looked at me and the laughter cracked out of her. She tried for a few moments to keep her hair from flying everywhere, then gave up and lifted her chin toward brilliant sky. I steered us onto a country road whose only obstacles to speed were an occasional tractor. I passed one like it was nothing more than a pothole.

She rose out of her seat and stood, holding onto the top of the windshield. Her hair went wild. "Know what I just decided?" she shouted.

"No—what?"

"I'm going to break up with Jim." She closed her eyes. There was her neck. Tan legs.

We were approaching a set of railroad tracks. I didn't want to slow down. I wanted to keep driving, never stop, just go. The seats were a warm hug. The car glided over the new pavement. We were almost at the tracks.

"Les," said Naomi. "Slow down." She sat and reached for her seatbelt.

The tracks sat atop a small hill. I knew we'd bottom out at best. I drove faster.

"Les!"

The front of the car scraped bottom on the way up, then lifted off the ground when it hit the tracks. The landing on the other side was a slam and we both jolted forward in our seats. Loose gravel made the road slippery as ice and we fishtailed. I did the worst and hit the brakes and we spun. The car tipped like it was about to turn over, but righted itself at the last second and dropped to a stop.

We sat in silence for a moment.

She spoke as if she were just waking. "Why did you do that?"

"I'm sorry" was all I could say. "I lost myself for a minute."

"But—why did you do that?"

I turned to her.

"You're bleeding," she said.

I felt like I needed to blow my nose, then looked down and saw my shirt. A red bloom of blood covered my chest. I took off my shirt and held it to my nose. "Are you okay?"

"I'm fine," she said. "We should probably move to the side of the road." Then, "Can you drive?"

"Yes." The car drove fine. I started back toward Boyd's. "I'm going to tell him a deer ran out in front of us, but I managed to avoid it."

When I got to Boyd's, he said, "What in God's name?"

I told Boyd about the deer and that I would pay for any damage he found, though I was pretty sure there was none. He was angry, but what could he say?

[*Les's full name is Leslie. It is one of the knots at the core of him, the fact that he has a traditionally female name. Obviously, there was teasing. Nowadays, most people in town call him Doc. The only person who uses Leslie is Nick Jennings at the hardware store. Nick had taken Joan on a date just before, in Nick's words, "Leslie swooped in and stole her." Whenever a stranger uses Les's full name, he tenses and says, "Just Les is fine."*

**You know, I'm beginning to resent these characterizations, mainly because this isn't how I'd describe myself and, frankly, I know myself best.**[2]

ACTUALLY, I'VE FOUND THAT THE PERSON WHO KNOWS YOU LEAST IS, WELL, YOU.[3]

**I should be in control of my own story.**

YOU ARE. YOU'RE TELLING THE STORY.

**But not in these brackets. I want to be out of the brackets.**

ARE YOU SURE ABOUT THAT? BECAUSE WHATEVER YOU SAY OUT OF THE BRACKETS CAN BE HEARD BY THOSE AROUND YOU. THE SAME GOES FOR ME. AND I'M NOT SURE YOU WANT THEM TO HEAR ME.

---

2   **I, Les, am writing in bold. I deserve a say.**

3   I, THE WRITER, HAVE FOUND THAT, IN ART AND IN LIFE, PEOPLE REACT WORST TO THE TRUTH THEY KNOW BUT ARE UNWILLING TO ADMIT.

**Go ahead and say whatever you want. I have nothing to hide.**

NOTHING? ARE YOU SURE ABOUT THAT? NOT, SAY, YOUR
LUNCHTIME ACTIVITIES?

. . . . . . . . . . . .

LES?

**You know what I *don't* need? I don't need another woman
controlling me.**

OH, COME ON, LES. YOU MUST LIKE BEING SURROUNDED
BY WOMEN. OTHERWISE YOU WOULDN'T HAVE SET YOUR
LIFE UP LIKE THAT.

**Sure. I planned to have a daughter.**

THERE ARE OTHER AREAS YOU COULD CONTROL, BUT
DON'T.

**Such as?**

SUCH AS FIRE LYNN AND HIRE A GUY.

***Fire* Lynn? And hire a *guy*? That's a laugh.**

MAYBE YOU WANT TO BE SURROUNDED BY WOMEN TELLING
YOU WHAT TO DO BECAUSE THE ONE WOMAN YOU WANTED
SO BADLY TO RUN YOUR LIFE, OR JUST TAKE THE SMALLEST
BIT OF INTEREST IN IT—YOUR MOTHER—NEVER DID.

. . . . . . . . . . . . ]

I dropped Naomi close to the office, not too close to be spotted, and
took the long way home. I thought I'd gotten myself steady, but when
I walked in the house and saw Joan on the couch in her bathrobe,
anger snapped in me like a ripped muscle. How I hated that bathrobe. Hated the faded peach terrycloth, hated how it drooped on her
skeletal frame.

"What happened?" asked Joan. "And why are you home?"

"I cleared my afternoon appointments to get ready for the party. I made a quick stop with the car and banged my nose." I went upstairs to our bedroom, threw open our closet doors, and pulled one of her dresses off its hanger.

"Here, Joan," I said, holding out the dress. "Why not put this on?"

She looked at it like it was poisoned.

"Come on, Joan." I put an arm around her shoulders and tried to get her to stand up from the couch.

She pushed against me with one arm. "Stop it!" She was stronger than I imagined.

I pulled at the tie of her robe and it opened, showing her bra and underwear.

She jumped up. "Hey!" she shouted. "Get your hands off me."

I reached to pull the robe off her shoulders and she smacked my hand away.

"If you touch me again—"

"What?" I said. "If I touch you, what?" I couldn't help myself. I was smiling. "I thought I was supposed to touch you. I'm your husband after all."

"Mom! Dad!" Carla came downstairs. "What is going on?"

Joan wrapped the robe around herself as tight as she could. "Your father has lost his mind."

"No," I said. "I've only lost my patience." I went to the kitchen and flung open the refrigerator door. "I'm going to make myself a hamburger. Anyone want one?"

"You know I don't eat meat, Dad," said Carla.

I could handle everything about Carla—the extra weight, the long, tie-dyed skirts, the patchouli, the vegetarianism, the bracelets—everything but the dreadlocks. They were ugly, like a heap of brown scouring pads, and dirty. Even worse, she sewed tiny bells into them, just to make sure they were seen and heard.

"Your loss." I slapped a patty on a plate.

Just inside the door was the CD player Joan kept on the counter. I unplugged it, brought it outside and turned it to the rock station. Joan hated rock. She only wanted easy listening or oldies.

"Don't ruin your appetite," yelled Carla after me. "I planned on cooking dinner."

I held up the spatula and shouted over the music. "Oh, no need to worry about me." The sun was directly overhead, focused, it seemed, directly on my bald spot. The air was thick and flies had already begun to dive in for a bite of raw meat.

I lit the grill. Its heat felt like sunburn on my face. I leaned into the heat as far as I could until I finally had to pull away.

[*As a child, Les knew the kitchen was the one place he could find his mother. He made sure he was there every day just before supper so he could spend time alone with her. Eventually, he took over the cooking while she flicked through the Montgomery Ward catalog. She didn't exactly teach him to cook as much as do so little he had to learn by trial and error. She told him what to change the next time he made a dish as she tasted bites between drags on her cigarette.*

**Not this horseshit again. If you keep this up—**

IF I KEEP THIS UP—WHAT, LES? WHAT ARE YOU GOING TO DO? REMEMBER, I KNOW *EVERYTHING*.

**I don't care. And I'm taking this out of the brackets.**

I WOULDN'T ADVISE THAT.

"No more brackets," I said and took a bite of burger. The grease dripped toward my chin and I wasn't about to wipe it off. I *love* grease.

The music stopped and a woman spoke from the radio: "Then I guess we need to talk about the porn."

"Yeah, c'mon. Let's talk about the porn." This actually felt good. I looked up at the sky and it was one of those days where a cloud traveled solo. Slow and with purpose, like it had somewhere to be, but at no particular time. It was just enjoying the ride.

"And how, at work, your computer screen used to face your office window, then, one day you clicked on a porn ad and quickly shut it. Then, the next day, you turned your computer around and were *very*, very busy at lunch. So busy you couldn't be interrupted."

I laughed and finished the last bite of burger. "Ever since, lunch has been the best part of my day."

Carla walked out from the kitchen, looking concerned. "Dad. What are you doing?"

"Oh, just talking about porn."

Her eyes widened and her face froze. She spoke through her teeth. "Dad, the neighbors. They can hear you."

"Who cares about the neighbors," I said. "They're all a bunch of assholes anyway." I picked up my plate and stood.

Carla's mouth fell open, then she said, "Dad? Are you okay?"

"Better than ever," I said and left, headed somewhere unknown. Then found myself at Radio Shack.

The next morning, I went to the garage to check that the twisted white streamers I'd hung the night before were still affixed to the ceiling. An oscillating fan rocked silver paper bells as it blew past.

"Hi, Dad." Carla jingled into the garage. She wore ankle bracelets that made her sound more like a belly dancer than a college graduate. She huffed past me carrying a fistful of silver and white balloons. Her cheeks crowded her eyes, making them disappear a little more each time I saw her. Every year that Joan grew skinnier, Carla inflated, as if she were eating for the two of them.

I followed Carla into the dining room where she let go of the balloons, which bumped against the ceiling milliseconds apart. Joan came down the stairs in her bathrobe.

We all stood staring at the balloons and then I said to Joan, "I have your present."

"Don't you want to save it for the party?" said Joan.

"Yeah, Dad," said Carla. "You can't open it before."

"Actually, it's something we can use at the party," I said. "Joan, I really think you'll like it. You should open it now."

She shrugged. "Okay, Les. If you really want me to."

"Great," I said and went to pull it out from under our bed where I'd hidden it the night before.

I handed Joan the wrapped boxes and she opened them, confused about what the gift actually was. I talked about how she could clip the iPod to the band of her pants and run with it. How light it was and how it wouldn't skip. That the music was already inside and she didn't need to put in a disc or a cassette.

"Well," she said, running a thumb over the face. "Thank you."

"And we can use it for the party today. See? I bought speakers. I put all the music on there, too." I'd spent the better part of the night downloading songs from the computer.

"I don't know, Dad," said Carla. "I already have all the CDs ready for the party."

I'd been so wrapped up in the iPod, I forgot about the CD player. I needed to get rid of it—couldn't risk the thing broadcasting all my secrets. "Trust me," I said. "This will be easier. You don't have to load CD after CD. It just keeps going through the songs."

Carla and Joan looked at each other and Carla said, "Sure, Dad. Whatever you say."

"Where is the CD player, anyway?" I asked.

"Dad. I've got it covered." Carla put her hands on my shoulders and started steering me toward the garage. "You're supposed to just show up to the party and have fun. Can you go get the paper? It'll keep you occupied and help you relax."

When Carla planned the party, she didn't think about how hot the garage would get, even with the air conditioning cranking from inside the house. I was sweating so much my shirt stuck to my back.

Joan sat next to me drinking gin and soda. Beyond Carla and the party, we had nothing to talk about.

"Good cake," I said for the third time.

She pulled the fork from between her lips, bowed her head in agreement.

"You look nice," I said. Carla bought her a new lavender suit, had the hairdresser style her hair.

"Nice?" she said.

"Yes, nice," I said. "Very pretty."

Joan smiled and waved to arriving guests. "Oh, hi," she whispered.

"Maybe we should greet people."

Across the room, Naomi leaned against the wood beams of the garage wall. She wore a short skirt and a tank top with a V-neck. Like most of the other guests, she was fanning herself with one of the church bulletins announcing our silver anniversary.

I left the table.

"Dad?" Carla surprised me. I turned to face her. "Are you going to dance with Mom?"

"When?"

"Now," she said. "I'm going to play your song."

"Our song?"

"Yes," she said. "Your song." She pointed at the CD player. "It's ready to go."

I stared at the CD player and thought maybe I could unplug it and toss it in the backyard before the song started. Or, more importantly, before it started to talk. I caught Naomi looking at me. "Sure," I said. "Fine."

Carla led a protesting Joan to the dance floor, then passed her to me. No music had started and, for an excruciating moment, all eyes were on us. We fashioned stiff smiles. I wondered if people could see my hair standing up at being that close to Joan. Finally John Lennon's piano began to play the first chords of "Imagine." "Happy anniversary," I said. She echoed me. We tried to look like we had so much to talk about we'd never fit it all in.

"Carla's done a wonderful job," she said.

"Wonderful." I lifted her hand and she twirled under my arm.

The song ended and I kissed Joan on the cheek. Her skin was cool. Another song started, drawing more couples to the dance floor at Carla's insistence. I left Joan standing there.

"Naomi," I said.

She finished her sip of wine and hugged me.

"Glad you could make it," I said. "Party wouldn't've been the same without you."

"I couldn't miss a party for you and Joan," she said. "You were practically my parents for a few years."

I cringed, not wanting to think of myself as anyone's father. I whispered to her, "Did you break up with Jim?"

"Not yet," she said. "I'm not sure."

"Why?" I leaned back so I could see her.

"It's a big decision. I need to be certain."

The song ended and another began.

"Would you like to dance?" I asked.

"Um." Her cheeks turned pink. "Sure." She looked behind her at the small group of high school friends who'd come to the party and slid her plastic cup of red wine onto a table.

We joined the swaying couples on the dance square. My heart jumped. Out of the corner of my eye, I saw Carla staring at us from my seat next to Joan. I had a firm hold on Naomi's waist.

"Well, do you think you'll switch to optometry?" I asked.

I imagined us, side by side in our white coats, conferring about difficult cases. Of course, she'd be an apprentice, so I'd do most of the coaching in the beginning. We'd live somewhere like Florida, where sunlight warms the sea air. And where, at night, a salty breeze would make white curtains dance as we made love. We'd spend Sunday mornings in our pool or on the beach. Drive convertibles. Drink cappuccinos. Read the paper naked in bed.

Naomi pulled her body from mine, leaned against my arm.

"I don't think so," she said. That must not have been her first cup of wine. She stumbled. I recovered and kept her steady. Her teeth had turned gray. "I need something a little more exciting. And all those cranky old people. I couldn't stand it."

A single drop of sweat crept toward my elbow. I felt as if the lights in the room had just been turned on. All of the other couples on the dance floor crowded the small space. The heat of their bodies felt suffocating to me.

"The old people," she'd said. "It's like they'd want to suck the youth out of me and keep it for themselves."

I guided Naomi around the border of the parquet floor. She was having a hard time keeping up.

"Are you okay?" I asked after she stumbled a second time.

"Totally fine." She laughed through her nose.

The music stopped.

"Thanks for the dance, Les." She hugged me.

Another song began. It was faster, more upbeat. "Rock This Town" by the Stray Cats.

"How about one more," I said.

She frowned. She opened her mouth to speak.

"You're out here already."

She turned to her friends at the wall. "Guess it can't hurt," she said, then slid her hand into mine.

I pulled Naomi along to the beat. For every two of my steps, she took one. I twirled her. She couldn't untwist her feet and nearly fell. I caught her, helped her regain her balance.

"Dad?" Carla was standing next to us, staring at Naomi.

"What, dear?" We rocked side to side keeping time with the music. Well, I was keeping time to the music.

"Dad? What are you doing?"

I spun Naomi to arm's length and back. "Dancing," I said. "What does it look like I'm doing?"

"Making a fool of yourself," said Carla.

I double stepped away from her toward the opposite side of the dance floor. We were closed in on one side by the tables.

"Les," said Naomi. Her voice was impatient.

I held her tight, leading us both in circles. Faster and faster, my feet shuffled us from one end to the other. I was practically carrying her by then. I took her right hand in mine. With all my strength I jerked her away from me and let go.

She crashed into a table and fell on the cement floor.

"Les!" screamed Joan.

The song continued, but everything else stopped. No one lifted so much as a spoon.

"She's had too much to drink." I walked to her, touched her shoulder. "Naomi? Are you okay?"

She slapped my hand away. "I'm fine."

Joan came around the table. "Why don't you go put on a dry shirt," she said to me. She bent to Naomi. "I'll take care of her." A lily in Joan's corsage brushed Naomi's cheek.

The music stopped. A moment of silence, then the woman's voice began, *Les never was a dreamer until he became an adult. Before that, it was all black and white—meeting one goal, then another, ticking off boxes on the To-Do list of life. But when life took a route he didn't like, little by little his imagination became his reality.*

Everyone in the garage turned in their chairs, even lifted off their seats and craned their necks to find the source of the voice.

*But living in your imagination is dangerous, isn't it, Les? Ask your sister. If you live in it for too long, you can't switch back. You lose perspective on where fantasy stops and reality begins.*

I focused on the door to the kitchen and walked toward it. Just in front of it was the CD player. I unplugged it, but the voice kept talking.

*Les has been fantasizing about moving to Florida with Naomi. Starting an optometry practice with her and—other things. A whole new life. A fresh start. A second chance at youth.*

I grabbed the CD player and walked to our bedroom. The curtains were closed. The room smelled of baby powder. And yet, underneath the talcum, I could smell the hours upon hours of sleep—moldy bread and sour hair. Draped on the foot of the mattress was Joan's bathrobe. I wrapped it around the CD player.

*But there are no second chances at youth, are there, Les?*

I headed outside through the kitchen and turned on the grill. The gas roared into flame. A few curious people had come into the kitchen from the garage to see what I would do next. I waved at them. Maybe I *would* go to Florida. Alone.

I stuffed the CD player and the bathrobe inside the grill and closed the lid. The voice became muffled, but kept going until the entire grill went up in flames. Right then, I should have gone to the car and kept driving until I reached saltwater. But something happened with Joan. She took charge and herded everyone away from the back porch. She told everyone thanks very much for coming, but the party was over. A couple of the guys threw water on the grill, but that only made things worse. The flames came back with a vengeance.

"Turn off the gas," said my friend Ken.

When I went to reach for the valve, I couldn't get close. The heat was like a wall I couldn't move beyond.

"Everyone out!" said Ken.

I backed away into the yard just as the deck started to catch fire, then ran to the end of the drive. A group from the party had gathered across the street. Others were driving away. Naomi was getting into the passenger seat of a car. Carla was hugging Joan, who'd broken down crying. The town's fire siren wound up and started its ebb-and-flow alarm. A fire truck blared its horn and pulled right up into the yard. I walked past the truck and through the yard behind it so I could see how far the fire had spread.

For a split second, it was as if the flames sucked in all the air and sound. Everything was silent—the birds stopped chirping, the fire truck's hum grew distant, like we were underwater in a sheltered cove. Then, *boom*! When I opened my eyes, I was on the grass, covering my head. The firefighters were shouting at one another.

One came up to me, impatient, and asked, "Is anyone inside?"

"No," I said.

"Are you sure?"

I took a moment. "No, I'm not sure."

He jogged toward the two guys manning the hose, put on his oxygen mask. Another guy followed and they went inside.

In the end, no one was injured. Everyone had cleared out before the fire reached the house. After the fire squad left, Joan and I ducked through the new hole in the breakfast nook wall, squished across the carpet, in shock at everything that was ruined. Water drops plunked on our scalps and traveled down the napes of our necks. It wasn't the fire that did the most damage. It was the water. Carla's senior picture, the TV, all the electronics, the walls, the carpet. Joan called the insurance company, which sent out a team of guys who dealt with water damage. The guys came in like a pit crew and started crowbarring door frames from the wall and ripping up carpet, sledgehammering the walls. The foreman saw Joan, close to tears, watching them and said, "Hey, guys, let's work on the siding for a bit." And the guys nodded and took their crowbars and ladders outside.

I sat down in one of the dry armchairs in the front room and Joan went upstairs. When she came down, she was carrying a suitcase she'd packed for the two of us.

"We'll stay at your mom's tonight," she said. "I don't want to hear it from my parents."

When we got to Mom's, Joan guided me to the couch by the elbow and brought me a cup of tea, which I drank. Then, for the first time in as long as I could remember, she put her arm around me. She walked me to the spare room, told me to get some rest.

We no longer had our RV, but Ken let us park his camper in our driveway until the house was fixed. I thought we'd hate being inside that tiny camper and we did for the first day or so, like it was a shirt that fit too tight across the shoulders. But after a couple days, we got used to eating and sleeping in the same space and Joan even said to me, "It's not so bad. Being in here."

The Thursday following the party, I stepped inside the camper, expecting it to be empty. To my surprise, Joan was there.

"Why aren't you running?" I asked.

She showed me the front page of the local paper and told me she'd waited for me so we could read about the fire together.

# The Widow Complex

WHENEVER WE'RE on the swings in the backyard, near the dark wood fence that my wife and I call the Black Widow Condo Complex, I quiz my daughter, Marissa, on spiderwebs.

"What kind of web is this?" I ask, pointing to one with a pattern.

"A regular spider's," she says. "Not a widow."

"Right," I say. "And that?" I hold my son in the crook of my arm and, with my other hand, I block Marissa from getting too close. I show her quickly what I want her to name, bring my hand back.

"A widow egg sack."

It looks like a miniature Chinese lantern made of onionskin with taffy pulls all over. Or a lone barnacle.

"Very good," I say. "And how is a widow's web different from a regular web?"

"A regular web goes round and round. A widow's web goes back and forth. All over." She draws zigzags with her finger, still chubby at the base.

"Or—?"

"Or it's like a sail, except the sail is at the bottom like the trampoline at gymnastics, not straight up."

At Halloween we walked past homes decorated with the usual pumpkins, witches, ghosts. One house had fake webbing stretched over bush branches, no pattern, nearly opaque with random strands.

"What kind of web is that?" I asked Marissa.

"Widow," she said. "Widows are black or brown."

If I flip over my daughter's tricycle or my son's plastic scoot car, between the wheel and axle or under the seat are the remnants of an earwig, a skein of disconnected strands waving loose in the breeze, an empty egg sac.

I once saw a television show where a man in Australia shoved his foot into a boot he'd left in his garage and got bit by a huge recluse. The foot necrosed, then he died. Now, if I leave a pair of shoes outside, I give them two good shakes, slap the toe, look into the cave of it. Even then, as I push my foot in, it feels like I'm living on the edge.

Yesterday I was hosting a playdate, carrying a stack of small plastic bowls, different colors: preschool blue, sour apple, grape candy. Inside one bowl were four unwanted raspberries and, in the others, droplets of water. We adults could have shared from one bowl, but not three preschoolers. No, they had to have their own bowls, each a different color and each called out like a Saturday-night order at a bar. "Green! I want green!" If a child doesn't get the color commanded, he will hop in place, heels pounding the floor, fists pumping and we adults will panic—what to do? give in or hold firm?—and the host always gives in, always, because the host is most concerned with being a good host. Which, like I said, was me.

As far as these playdates go, there must be three adults present at all times, never less. Because I'm the lone man, I can't meet with just one woman. Even the term—play*date*.

We made our way inside from the front yard. One of my wife's friends walked behind me. We were talking in the disjointed way parents who're half watching kids do. "And so, you think she's ready for kindergarten? It's Evelyn's turn, Marissa! Let her have the tricycle. You have to share." That pause of silence while Marissa begrudgingly gave up the tricycle she didn't want to play with until she saw Evelyn grab it. "And so, kindergarten. Yeah. Not until she's there socially"—when I felt a spike of pain like an IV needle plunged deep in my thigh.

A couple weeks ago, I opened our mailbox, reached for the pile, felt the stick of threads and pulled my hand back. I lowered to eye level—hers—afraid the widow would be up front, ready to launch like a flying squirrel. But she was in the back, suddenly awakened by the blast of light, readying her legs—nimble when free of her abdomen's weight—to repair her trap. I thought about killing the widow but hesitated. As long as she stayed in her corner, what was the harm?

A few days later, I opened the mailbox and saw another spider walking on the side wall, one slow step, one leg at a time, toward her.

"Turn back, buddy," I said. "Bad idea."

Then the next day, I pulled out the mail and there he was, a thin, limp skeleton on top of a credit card offer.

Day after day, I'd see a spider creeping toward the back and the next day, its skeleton would be smashed or wedged or hanging loose in the mail stack. Then she built a web screen around herself to hide behind. Every day, another skeleton, another spider stepping careful to its death. Soon she grew too big for the screen and moved to the opposite corner, no longer concerned about whether she could be seen or not. They came anyway.

Once I put my son in his bucket swing out back. The swing's chain ends in a metal triangle that attaches to the seat through a channel like an empty door hinge. My son was still young, maybe four months, so I sat in front of him and pushed with my fingertips while I drained a beer. Marissa twisted on the swing next to us.

After a while, I saw the bunch of white thread in the metal channel where the chain attaches to the swing. I stood, put my beer high, stopped the swing by the chain, lifted him out as if he were a fibula in the game of Operation, set him ten feet away on the grass, told Marissa to get next to him, and peered into the channel. The spider was in there, though I wasn't sure if she was dead or alive. I found a stick. My hand shook. I stood as far away as I could, then stabbed the stick into the empty space.

The spider came out the other end, sprinted across the top of the swing, front legs high, challenging me to a duel. Brown recluse. I pulled off my flip-flop and slammed it on the swing. The baby cried. Marissa shouted, "Daddy! Dad!" The spider fell to the grass.

"Stay back!" I said. The baby was crying so hard I knew I'd have snot to wipe. Then Marissa. "Dad! Where is it? Daddy! Did you kill it? Dad!"

I lifted my bare foot, hopped, then planted it atop my other. I bent to study the grass. Then I saw her, scrambling, hiked front legs: *I'm coming for you, bastard.*

I pounded the grass with my shoe, trying to back away, but not able to reach past a certain point, then stopped myself and watched the spider curl into death.

"Dad! Dad! Did you get it, Dad?"

My previous self had a PhD. I still have the degree, of course, just not the drive to keep up the constant churn of dissection. I acknowledged too late my hatred for literary theory. When I finally stepped away from the pomp and circumstance, I understood that literary theory did to books what gross anatomy did to bodies. I'd come to dread lifting the cover of a new book, which, at one time, had been my favorite thing in the world. The classes were less a time for debate and discussion and more about title dropping every book ever written and, more importantly, who could be most clever at kissing the professor's ass. When one professor walked in with a manicure, rubbing his thumb back and forth over his other polished nails all through class, it sent me over the edge. *Pretense.* I thought. *The point of the degree isn't academic. It's to prove how far the distance from primitive man. When, in truth, we're all cavemen. We want a comfortable home, hot food, and sex. That's it.*

My wife's body is what I saw first when we met. It was perfectly hourglass and she knew how to show it off without showing too much. After two kids, she still looks damn good, more like a woman, but she doesn't see it that way and, consequently, I don't see her much anymore, let alone touch her.

She has these ideas about how my cupping her breast or grabbing her ass is treating her like an object, but really, I just want to feel the warmth that was so easy and uncomplicated before we brought two other people into our relationship. She says I'm trying to put her in her place, to assert my power over her because of the situation I'm in, how powerless I can sometimes feel about my own life.

Who knows, maybe she's right. But in the moment when I reach for her, I can say with all honesty, I'm not thinking of anything but being close to her.

My wife might as well get on a plane every day and fly to

Istanbul, that's how distant our worlds. Every morning, she show-ers, dresses, makes herself up, and goes off into the world, while I heat bottles, pick up browned banana half-moons from the carpet, offer a snack, change a diaper, push dirty clothes into the wash-ing machine, offer snack, diaper change, push wet clothes into the dryer, preschool, grocery shop, snack, diaper, meal prep, swim class, diaper, snack, park trip, doctor visit, diaper, snack, control rage as kids throw uneaten dinner at the floor and walls, bath, diaper, snack, books, bottle.

Repeat.

When my wife comes home from work, she hugs the kids, every once in a while she hugs me, then she sits at the kitchen table like a ripped squeeze toy, quiet and empty. She is always genuinely ap-preciative of the dinners I cook, and compliments me on what great food I make, saying she could never do what I do.

Since the bulk of what I do is provide food and wipe clean its remnants, I now wonder if I should have gone to culinary school. Most days my biggest struggle is what would I rather. Stand up, walk out the door, and never once look back or drop neck first from the doorframe.

Every other month when a huge deal is closing, she works week-ends, too. By the second Sunday, I'm at cliff's edge and I haul the kids to the pizza joint where Marissa runs squealing between the long wooden tables, annoying everyone who doesn't have a young child in tow. My son sits on my thigh, staring at the blinking lights of video games and I drink a pint. Without fail, some woman will approach me and say one of the following:

"You teach jiujitsu at Westside Martial Arts, right? I see you through the window on Tuesday mornings before my bikrim yoga class."

"Oh my God, you're the early morning weatherman. Can we take a picture with you?"

(Because nothing makes some women more uncomfortable than a man without a job, so they just go ahead and assign me one.)

"Daddy Day Care today, huh? Letting Mom have a break?" Then gives me a smile normally reserved for a young child and may even go so far as to pat my upper arm.

About the forty-first time the Daddy Day Care comment came around, I looked dead serious at the woman and said, "I normally never help. I mean raising kids is a woman's job, right? But she got her period today, so here we are." I finished the last half of my beer as the woman stood there staring, gape-mouthed, then I winked, raised my glass, and said "cheers."

Of course, there's the other end of the spectrum where I get the long end of the stick and all the credit for being a great parent. A lone man with two kids in the grocery store will get no less than five *attaboys* between the milk aisle and the checkout stand.

Whereas, the way my wife tells it, a mother in the same situation hears how beautiful or cute or well-behaved her kids are. Never a compliment to her. Because what else is there to her? As if by bearing a child, her own body has ceased to exist and has nothing more to offer the world.

My wife is a principal in an advertising agency, which means she's the most stylish person within a ten-mile radius of our suburban desert town. This isn't much of a problem for her since she grew up in New York City, one of the things that drew me—a small-town Ohio guy—to her. It seemed so exotic, growing up in the big city. Then, after a while, I realized kids in a big city end up making their own small town of it, that they drink cheap beer outdoors, too (in parks, not fields like us country kids) and scuttle away when cops make an appearance.

My wife can make the blandest gray dress look like the most stylish outfit you've ever seen. Maybe it's her—she elevates anything she puts on. Or maybe it's like a college major, something she's studied and perfected over the years. She's always a step ahead of every trend. "For every action, there is an equal and opposite reaction," she says. "All you have to do is look at what's going on now and do the opposite." Then she smiles and says, "The trick is to do it first. But don't tell anyone. It's the secret ingredient in my style recipe."

What I really fell in love with was her laugh. It's completely free and wild. When she laughs, she's no longer a grown woman, but a girl without responsibility or cares and I get to spend those brief moments with that girl.

One night in bed, she was reading *W Magazine*, which is the size of legal paper, but wider. Basically, she needs a music stand to read the monster so her arms don't get tired. She dropped the magazine to her lap and said, "Jeff Pardo is getting divorced for the second time."

She broke the quiet right as I was falling asleep, so I answered with a "hmmm."

"He said his first divorce was easier, even though they had kids. They were both reasonable, and, in the end, just friends who grew apart. They worked out the custody agreement without any drama. The money. All that." She picked up the magazine again. "The second wife, he says, wants everything she can get. And they were only married two years."

I was awake by then and pushed a hand under my head. "I suppose if that happened with us, I'd move out and get an apartment. You could keep the house."

"No," she said and flipped a page. "We'd sell the house and split it."

The hardest part of being a full-time dad is that dudes only get together to *do* something. So even though I know other guys in the same boat as me, we don't meet up much. Unless we're riding a bike or playing racquetball, climbing, skateboarding, dribbling a soccer ball or basketball, throwing a football, golfing, swinging a bat, essentially anything that involves a ball—we aren't spending an afternoon together. A friend and I tried tennis once because at least the kids were contained in the court, but a lob to a tiny shoulder blade put an end to the match. Not to mention it was summer in the desert—bad idea, even if the court's shaded. Walk outside in the summer and the heat is an instant headache that drains a body's energy one sweat drip at a time.

And then I think friendships are too complicated at this age. I'm happy just hanging out with my kids. They're my best friends, and, really, who needs more than two friends? The kids and I get a cup of ice cream and sit on a bench in the shade to people watch. My daughter next to me, holding her plastic spoon with a pinky lifted, which fascinates me because it isn't learned. The pinky lift must be tied to a specific gene on the female DNA. And then there's my boy with his spoon in his fist. Marissa taking careful bites and my son with those wide-spaced teeth toddlers have, ice cream like a goatee and we're quiet, just eating, and every once in a while my son will say "puppy" or "hi!" to a passing airplane and, in between, his sounds of contentment, which are different than babbling, somewhere between singing and talking. Babbling is practice talk, loud and precise. Sounds of contentment are more like pigeon coos, half sound, half air. Then my daughter wipes the corners of her mouth and lifts her ice cream cup with her thumb and middle finger and drops it in the trash. She leans into my free leg and drops her head against my ribs and I'm hers and she's mine. And I know then I'll never leave her. It is she who will leave me.

The dregs of the day, 5 to 8 p.m.—those hours are the hardest. That's when I look at the clock every four minutes and wonder if bedtime will ever arrive. And, as I was carrying the kids' stack of bowls, we were up against the dregs, which is why the playdates, to distract us all from "How long till bed?"

I felt the needle pierce of pain, and my mind went black for a nanosecond, as if a movie were starting, and then it was all there—the mailbox, the skeletons, the webs, the papery egg sacs, the swing, the tricycle, the shoes, the Black Widow Condo Complex. I pitched the bowls, beat my own thigh, the bowls ricocheted off the house and my wife's friends shouted "What! What is it?" and my back hit the ground, my son crying, the preschoolers too scared to speak and I yelled, "Where is it? Where? Do you see?" still slapping my leg and finally I calmed down and Karen spotted a lump of brown on the cement. She moved close and said, "It's a bee." I saw it wasn't moving, that I must have killed it mid-apeshit. My head fell back and I remembered that, soon after the widow came out of hiding and moved to the opposite side of the mailbox, the spiders stopped coming. A couple days later, I searched for her in the dark corner with the strange hope one reserves for the underdog. I figured she could kick open the mailbox with a single leg by then, that she'd probably left for a bigger place with a view. I found her, though, and stared for a few moments, waiting for movement, but she hung limp—dead from starvation.

# Last Chance

A COUPLE months after my big fight with Luanne I got lost in thought and found myself fifty feet from the trailer I once called home. One second I was following a tractor, itching to pass, the next second—there it was, boarded up, rotting from the inside out. Death trap. Ever since the day of my real-life nightmare, I'd gone out of my way to avoid it. I would drive an extra fifteen minutes on country roads, past corn, soy, and wheat fields in order to block my view of what was essentially a rusted dumpster. That day, when I caught sight of it, I slammed on the brakes and stared, unable to choose between turning around or driving past.

I finally decided I'd seen the place, what difference did it make? Keep going.

Can you believe, as I looked at it my first thought wasn't about my poor mom or my shitty dad, it was about that damn loaf pan? How the meatloaf had sat on our counter for days, festering, drawing flies. It was the pan that'd sparked the fight between my mom and dad, and the fact that I'd never returned it to Luanne—that was what she threw in my face during the argument.

Minutes later I found myself in Luanne's driveway. How'd I get there from the trailer? I had no memory of the drive. The garage was open, her truck inside. I went to her front door. I was sure she'd slam it in my face, if she even opened the door at all. I rang the bell and moved to the corner where she couldn't see me.

"What," she said.

"I remember the loaf pan."

"Good for you. Go get yourself a cookie." She almost closed the door, but I stopped her.

"The pan—it might still be in the trailer."

"I don't care about the goddamn pan."

"Yes, you do."

"It's been twenty-five years. The pan's long gone, May."

"The trailer's been boarded up ever since what happened. There's a chance."

She puffed a laugh. "That place would fall down on our heads as soon as we stepped inside."

"Maybe," I said. "Maybe not."

"Why do you want me to go? Bring Roger."

"I can't bring Roger."

"Oh, baloney."

"You're the only one."

"The only one what?"

"Who's seen that part of me."

"So go show Roger."

"I can't."

She folded her arms. "He's your husband. Show him who you really are."

"Okay," I said. "But I need you to go with me first."

"What? Why am I even talking to you?" She flicked up her hands. "I'm mad at you."

"Because you can't help yourself. And neither can I. So let's get this over with already."

I turned and walked to my car. I was sure she'd follow me. She was too curious not to. I knew the pan was in there. I could feel its pull.

Friendships that span decades can appear complicated at arm's length, but up close, they're more like a favorite blanket or teddy bear from childhood. Maybe there's only a scrap left, maybe it's been lost forever, or in a few rare cases, it's treasured and cared for, within reach when you need it. In a friendship that endures, there's no wool to pull, because the person knows you, whether you like it or not. She understands what makes you interesting and unique— why you were friends in the first place. She also remembers the unsavory bits. But the happy part of reviving a lost friendship is that you push all those annoying traits aside. At first. Then the frustrations creep in, a little at a time, and you're both back to being plain. old. you. *Take me or toss me*, you both eventually say, in so many words. Sometimes, that's when the friendship truly begins. When you both no longer give a holy hoot. And sometimes that's when the friendship breaks forever.

Luanne and I hit our make-or-break moment in the middle of a party. I was elbow deep into hosting yet another Pampered Chef shindig, when I drew a line in the sand and walked straight out. My own house. Luanne was up there hawking the pizza stone again— always the frigging pizza stone, I mean these women all had the pizza stone. Try something new!—when I slammed down my serving tray and left the house. I must have walked for over an hour. It took that long to stuff my own anger back in its cage.

The cars were all gone when I came home. All except hers. I

exhaled, pinched the bridge of my nose, said, "Might as well get it over with." Went inside like nothing, like I'd just stepped out to haul the trash.

"What in God's green earth happened to you, May?" said Luanne. "I had to handle everything here by myself. The service, the pitch, the orders, the cleanup."

"Luanne? My only response to that is: it's about time."

I wanted to wring May's neck for walking out on me in the middle of a party. Of course, she blamed her meltdown on me.

"You never help," she whined. "I do everything and you take all the credit. And the money."

"Oh, please," I said. "Go lie to someone who'll believe you."

I'm sure she told anyone who'd listen that she was the one who threw all the parties. And in that she's telling the truth. But she *wanted* to throw all the parties. Volunteered. So much so that I stopped asking and just slapped her address on the invite every time. Don't be fooled, she puts on a good show. *I have to be careful about how I present myself around town. I'm a teacher. I'm judged for what I do outside the classroom, too.*

That's what she wanted. To be judged. She wanted everyone to see her big, fancy house and decide that she was just as fancy. But there's no fooling me. I know she came from dirt. I know everything.

"What's that supposed to mean, *it's about time*?"

"You know exactly what I mean. Why am I the only one throwing the parties here?"

"Because you *want* to throw the parties. You want everyone to see your expensive furniture and your 'custom' house. 'We built the house ourselves. It was a labor of love, but it was worth it.' Barf."

"You're so transparent. Could you be any more jealous?"

I dropped a dish in the sink mid-scrub. What the hell did I care about cleaning up? "You wish I was jealous. At least I got my first choice for a husband. Unlike you, who reminds poor Roger every day he'll never live up to the god who was Michael."

"See, there you're wrong. Michael *was* your first choice."

"Until you stole him!"

"I didn't steal him. He ran to me. Couldn't wait to get away from you."

"I was your only friend for *years*. Years! And what do you do to repay me? Steal my boyfriend."

"*He* broke up with *you*. I didn't steal him."

"You did. You orchestrated the whole thing. And you know what else you stole? My mom's loaf pan! That was an heirloom. My mom cooked a meatloaf and I brought it into that hellhole and you never thanked us and never returned the pan."

"I have no clue what you're talking about."

"Yes, you do. You ate banana bread out of that pan all the time. It was green with scalloped edges!"

"Can you even hear yourself? You're not making any sense. Take control."

"Oh, I'm taking control. Right now. I don't ever want to see your face again."

"Good luck with that. We each have a daughter in majorettes, remember?"

"Even that you had to steal! I couldn't be a majorette without you elbowing your way onto the squad. *I'm going to twirl with fire! It'll be a hit!*"

"And there you were, being your usual bore self, wondering why you weren't the star. Blubbering about Michael breaking up with you, twirling the same routine. Do something shocking! Amaze people!"

"Yeah, well, I'd rather be a good person than an entertaining one."

"Maybe that's your problem."
"Maybe that's yours."

Can you indulge me for a minute? Would you just look at the invitation Luanne sent?

Where can I possibly start? I mean, are we German now, capitalizing nouns? The apostrophes. The font. The reply options. What really popped my cork, though, was the "gourmet food made by Your's Truly." First of all, everyone knows *I'm* the one cooking the food. That's what they come for! Not the gadgets.

No one wants them anymore. They want the dang free lunch! To top it all off, I'm an English teacher. Run the invitation by me so I can at least proofread. And right there I hit the nail on the head. That's exactly why she didn't want me to proof the invite. Because she didn't want me correcting her. Because I graduated from college and she didn't. Because somewhere along the line, we switched income brackets.

You would think that after everything that happened with May, what with her dad being in prison and all, she'd've grown quieter and more withdrawn at school after the incident. But no. It was just the opposite.

She moved in with her aunt, her hair got bigger, her clothes brighter, her laugh louder.

"If I'm going to be the town cautionary tale, I might as well fucking embrace it." She lit a cigarette for me. She'd convinced me no one would notice us out back behind the cafeteria dumpster. She was right. We went there every day at lunch. "Besides they all want to get close to me. Like I have a wild gene they want to be the first to discover, see if they recognize it in themselves."

It was true. I'd been her only friend for years and now she had more friends than she knew what to do with. But I was the girl she talked to one on one. Everyone always wanted to find out where she went at lunch. She told them she walked home. Her aunt's yard bordered the school parking lot. No one asked me where I went.

For the longest time, May had been my secret. Sure, we were friends, but I didn't exactly announce it. She came over to my house and we kept a distance at school. But then, after the murder, our friendship flipped somehow, and I became her secret.

Me. A secret.

No, I'm not the type of girl anybody needs to hide.

"Always look smart, May," Aunt Helen said to me as a child. We were crossing the street to the portrait studio. The fabric of our gloved hands grew hot from the friction of such a tight grip. "We're outsiders in this town. A spinster and her orphan niece. So you must always look smart."

Every year, from as far back as I could remember, Helen had taken me to sit for pictures. Before, it'd been a treat, getting dolled up in a pretty dress, but after everything that happened with Mom and Dad, I didn't want to look at pictures of myself. Before, the smile had been real, because I got to pretend for a day that I was the girl in the picture. A real smile on a pretend girl. But the pictures had become a chore because the smile was no longer real.

I had dragged my feet getting ready for the pictures. Earlier that day, I'd been exploring the creek with my friend Roger. He said he'd found worms the size of his thumb there and had caught a huge catfish with one. If Helen knew about the mud and the worms I'd never be able to see Roger again, so Roger and I rinsed our arms and legs at his house.

"Little May," said the photographer. "Not so little anymore." He bent to my height, licked his thumb and cleared a mud streak I'd missed from my hairline.

We never had any kids, Roger and I. We tried. For a long time we tried, but it just didn't happen. So we built the house instead.

I can't help but feel I failed him. Some days I want to say, *Go off and find yourself a new wife. A younger one. Have a family.* And other days I'm selfish and think, *Don't leave us. Not twice. We can't be left twice.* Tiffany calls him Dad and maybe that's enough. He says I'm silly, that he's perfectly happy with our daughter. See? He calls her "our daughter." But I know there's a place deep inside he won't show me, where the flame burns for a child of his own.

Michael and I got married just before Tiffany arrived. I was enormously pregnant at the wedding, but I didn't care. At the time, everyone thought we were rushing into things. But two years later, when he died in a car accident, I was glad we followed our own timetable and no one else's.

A few weeks after the accident, my aunt Helen rushed into my bedroom before church.

"Get out of bed." She scurried around the room picking up tissues and gathering clothes.

I hugged my pillow and hoped she'd leave.

"You're a single mother now," she said. "A threat."

"What are you talking about?"

"You're a threat to the women in this town. They'll get ideas in their heads that you live solely to seduce their men." She threw the pile of clothes into the hamper. "You're a threat to men, too. They don't like to see a woman making it on her own. They like to feel needed."

I propped myself up on my pillows. Tiffany stood in the doorway in a blue ruffled dress. She had the smoothest blonde hair—so silky it often unwound when I tried to braid it. Helen had twisted it into two tight braids and bound them with ribbons.

It was Tiffany's white gloves that got me out of bed.

May practically lived at my house as a kid. To the point where my parents joked about adopting her, and yet it wasn't far off. I went inside her house trailer exactly one time, when she was sick and my mom brought me over to deliver a meatloaf. My mom, always the class act, said she'd stay in the car while I ran the food in. Though I think Mom really wanted to see her, make sure she was okay. But she knew. It wasn't her place.

Just as I left the car, Mom said, "I should have taken that

meatloaf out of the pan and put it on a plate. That pan's an heir-loom, you know." I agreed. The pan didn't belong in that slump of a house. The aluminum was rusting from the ground up. The sides sagged. No driveway to speak of, just a few hops from the ditch. It looked like it fell off the side of a semi and was left for scrap.

I knocked on the door—barely—and saw May's dad on the couch.

"Come in," he said.

"Hi, Mr. Trame. My mom made some dinner for you."

"Why?"

"Well, I guess because May's sick."

He swiped an inhale off his cigarette and pointed at the kitchen with his head. "Put it over there." He wasn't watching TV or doing anything, really, besides smoking.

"How's May?" I asked.

"Same."

"Okay, well. Goodbye."

He nodded and I left, never so happy to get through a door in my whole life.

"How's she look?" asked Mom.

"Sick," I said.

"Well, of course, but—"

"She'll be better soon. Her dad said thank you for the food." Anything to get us off and away as fast as possible.

Mom looked relieved and started the car.

Not long after, May's dad shot and killed her mom. We never got our pan back.

What happened with the pan was this. I was sick with mono, which in itself had set my dad off. "That's the kissing sickness," he said. "Who'd you kiss?"

"No one," I said.

"You're a bad liar," he said. "At least you didn't inherit that from your mom. She's a world-class liar." He ran a hand over his stubble. "Just don't turn into a whore like her."

I was in bed for days, didn't even know Luanne had stopped in, when Mom came back after being gone for nearly a week. She up and left the second day I was terribly sick.

"I can't take this anymore," she said. "I was meant for bigger things than living on the side of a ditch."

She came in like nothing, like she'd gone out for cigarettes and forgotten our address, and went right to the meatloaf. Dad sat on the couch smoking like he was blind and hadn't seen her step through the door.

"Disgusting! Who the hell leaves meat on the counter to rot? Are those maggots?"

Dad jumped up and raged and the fight started, which was my cue to go to my room. I stared at a picture of myself in a fancy dress and white gloves and wished I was that girl. Then there was the gunshot and the smell of gunpowder and me alone with my mom, frantic while she bled to death.

"May. Baby. Help me." The shaking started from her hands and moved up her arms. Her mouth turned white. That's where death begins. In the lips.

The women came to our "Bargain Shop Till You Drop" party not for the 15 percent discount, but to get the story on what exactly happened between Luanne and me. Gossip straight from the source was their free gift. They knew we hadn't spoken in months, then all of a sudden there's an invite—from me. I never sent the invites. That was Luanne's department. What gives?

Luanne did end up going to the trailer with me that day. It

took me a while to find a wellspring of courage before I could even get out of the car. Luanne softened when she saw me shivering as I faced the box that contained the worst day of my life. I didn't know if I could open it.

"Come on." Luanne took my hand and walked me up the rusted, metal stairs.

For the party, we made sure the women had no choice but to stop at the Heirloom Table. Our inside joke. There were only two things on the table: a studio portrait of me that Luanne had found in my old bedroom. After we'd kicked our way inside, Luanne made her way down the hall and shoved open the warped door of my room, where she found the photo, water-damaged and curled in on itself.

"Toss it," I told Luanne when she showed me. But she tucked it in her purse, flattened it, and put it in a silver frame.

And then, of course, the other piece on the table was the loaf pan, chipped where it had come to rest on the floor during that horrible argument all those years ago. As we stood inside the front room of the trailer, we paused and took everything in. Luanne saw it first. The pan, still there, on its side, dropped like yesterday's fortune.

# The Key

I HAVE a couple friends in school who are latchkey kids like me. We all know—better than the kids who spend their afternoons with someone—what it's like to be scared of our own houses. A creak, a sudden knock, the snap of an icicle will send us running. Where to, we aren't sure. We just sprint. The big difference between me and those friends is that all of their parents are alive. I'm the only one whose dad is dead.

My friends and I get on separate buses at the end of the day. We wave goodbye as we ride away from each other. I'm on the bus headed home when I catch sight of the crooked pine at the corner of my street. Every time I see that tree, my body starts a countdown of the exact number of seconds I need to get to the bathroom. I move to the empty seat behind the driver so I'm ready. I stick my hand inside my coat to unfasten the key from the safety pin and—I can tell by how quickly the pin moves, how thin it feels—the key isn't there.

I hurry down the steps of the bus and cross the street. The cold makes the bones in my hands hurt. Fresh snow covers this morning's dull snow. It looks stiff and tricks me into thinking I can step on it, that, sure, I can take the shortcut across the yard—but I drop through. The skin of my ankle is wet. The wind is a burn.

I check under the rock and—no spare.

I'm on my front porch and I have to go so bad I can't hold it anymore. I grab a handful of pants and underwear and force it up my front so I can walk. I reach for the door and try the knob, even though I'm sure it's locked. The knob turns. I pull my hand away, like it's been stung.

Did I forget to lock the door this morning? I'm not completely sure because this morning seems like any other. But then I remember—Jimmy, the push-ups. I was in a rush. The urge to get to the bathroom is so strong I feel like I might throw up.

I open the door a crack, then a little wider. I search the dim for movement or a noise, but the house is quiet and still.

"Jimmy?"

Before school today my brother and I were in the kitchen and his muscles were out. Even though it's winter and Mom calls herself the heat miser, Jimmy refuses to wear a shirt. He says he's hot. I say he's showing off the muscles lined up on his stomach like straight teeth.

"Dawn," he said. "Watch."

He put an arm behind his back and did some quick push-ups against the table. Then he switched.

I looked at him like I couldn't have been more bored. "Big gym test today?"

He stood up and flexed, smiling huge, pleased with himself. He pulled a box of cereal from the cupboard and poured in a mouthful. He went to the fridge, got the milk and opened his lips just wide enough to add some. I checked the clock. Six minutes till the bus. Jimmy ate and smiled, milk running down the side of his chin.

"Who needs a bowl?" A piece of cereal flew from his mouth and landed in front of my orange juice.

"Gross," I said. "I have to leave now or I'll miss the bus."

I washed my glass in the sink and set it on the dish towel.

He was blocking me. I could've gone around, but if I did, he'd get annoyed and tease me and then I'd really be late.

"Whatever you do"—he chewed and chewed until he finally finished, then jabbed his finger at the front door—"do not open that fucking door when you're here alone." He wiped his chin. "Got it?"

I nodded.

He jiggled the window to make sure it was locked. "And don't forget the key."

About a month ago when Mom found me rinsing the hem of my pants in the laundry sink, she said, "Can't you wait till you're inside to go?"

"I do wait." I sprayed stain remover on the hems and rubbed. "Sometimes I forget the key and I hold it for as long as I can, then I just can't anymore. That's when I go behind the bush."

"What if someone sees you?"

"No one sees me."

Then she said, "It isn't that difficult, Dawn—to remember the key."

She didn't care about the key really. She only cared that her boyfriend, Mitch, and the neighbors knew her kids did dirty things like pee outside.

When Mitch moved in, Jimmy gave him a chance. They watched hockey together and talked about football. But little by little, Mitch started to act like he owned the place, like *we* were living in *his* house, instead of how it really was. First we couldn't eat macaroni and cheese for dinner because Mitch didn't like cheese, and pretty soon the only thing on TV was the news. Then what I think really set Jimmy off was that he took Jimmy's parking spot and Jimmy had to start parking off the alley in the back.

I complained to my brother that I didn't like Mitch being there. Jimmy only shrugged and said he wasn't home much and he'd be gone soon enough so what'd he care? But I knew my brother. Jimmy and Mitch pretended not to notice each other, but really they were like a pair of wrestlers circling, waiting for the first one to make a move.

One night after dinner, I passed Mitch reading the paper at the kitchen table and went in the bathroom. Just as I was pulling up my pants, he opened the door. I dropped and crossed my arms over my lap.

"Sorry," he said, shutting the door. "I didn't realize you were in here."

When I came out, he was back at the table reading the paper like nothing happened. Jimmy was at the sink washing a casserole dish. He glanced up at me. He knew same as me it was no accident. He went back to scrubbing and I made my way to the family room. Soon Mitch wandered in, sat in his chair, and turned on the news. Then Jimmy came in with his jaw twitching, went straight for the remote, and changed the channel.

It seemed like Mitch was going to let it pass, but then he said, "It's time for the news. Switch it back."

"What's so important that you have to know?" said Jimmy. "Isn't there anything else on TV? Dawn doesn't need to see this junk all the time. Murders and gas station robberies."

"Do you pay any of the bills in this house? Because I do," said Mitch. "I pay the cable bill and that means I will watch whatever I want. Turn on. The news."

"Oh, you pay one bill and think you run the place?"

Mitch leaned over and snatched the remote from Jimmy, who stood next to Mitch, arms crossed, smiling down at him. Then Mitch opened his can of pop.

"Diet pop is for pussies," said Jimmy.

Mitch jumped up from the chair, grabbed Jimmy by the T-shirt and slammed him against the wall.

"Do not call me that," Mitch said.

I saw in Jimmy's eyes he was going to beat Mitch to hamburger.

"Do it, Jimmy," I said.

They both looked at me.

"Do it."

Jimmy saw his chance and got an arm around Mitch's shoulders, kicked his legs out from under him, and slammed him on the ground so hard I heard the breath leave. Jimmy put Mitch in a headlock and started choking him, and Mitch bucked backwards in quick jerks, like a dog trying to escape its collar.

Mom rushed in from the kitchen and smacked Jimmy's head over and over, coming at him from both sides until he had to let go to defend himself.

If she weren't our mom, Jimmy would have punched her. He had his fist cocked like he was going to, but the thinking side of him snapped together and he realized it was his mom he was about to knock out.

I watched them, held tight, and a whisper came out of me that I couldn't stop. "Do it."

None of them heard me—the three of them were all shouting and arguing. Jimmy said if Mitch ever touched him again, he'd kill him.

"What kind of kids are you raising here? Threatening to *kill* me?"

Jimmy turned to Mom. "He walked in on Dawn in the bathroom. Tried to pretend it was an accident."

"It *was* an accident."

"No it wasn't," I said. I was enjoying this. Revenge. Finally.

"You're lucky Mom stopped me," said Jimmy. They were moving closer to each other, like the fight was about to start all over again. Mom got between them.

"You know what? I don't need this shit in my life."

"But you do need a house and you sure found yourself a good, free one here," said Mom.

"Free," said Mitch with a sneer. "You should pay *me* to put up with these kids."

"We're done," said Mom.

"Yes, we are," said Mitch. "He needs to leave. Why don't you go to one of your buddies' houses for the night? Get out and see what it's like on your own."

"I think we all know who's leaving," said Jimmy. "And it isn't me."

Mitch bent down, grabbed the remote, switched the TV back to the news, and sat down in his chair.

Jimmy and me looked at Mom, waiting for her to do something. She just threw up her hands and shrugged.

"Oh, no," said Jimmy. "Nope. You got two choices, Mitch. Leave on your own or wait till the cops get here." Jimmy grabbed the phone and started dialing. "Hi, yes," he said. "There's a guy in my house who beat me up and he's—"

Mitch rushed Jimmy. "Hang up that phone."

Jimmy sprinted across the room, away from Mitch. "He's trying to do it again." He gave them our address and ran outside.

Mitch yelled at Mom, "I can't believe you let him get away with that! If I was his dad, he'd've had his skull cracked a long time ago."

"The cops are going to be here soon," said Mom.

Mitch could see where things were headed. He grabbed his keys and slammed the front door so hard he shook the house.

A couple nights later I woke up to Mom and Jimmy whispering in the hall.

"What kind of noise was it?" said Jimmy.

"Like—" said Mom.

I got out of bed and peeked through my door. Jimmy's bedroom light was on. Mom was wearing her thin, blue nightgown, the one that shows too much. I wished she would give the nightgown away or throw it in the trash.

"Like a pop can opening," she said.

Jimmy and Mom stared at each other. Mitch. Every night after dinner, the TV then, *sss-snap*.

Jimmy held a knife. The handle was the color of my ugly garnet birthstone. The blade was curved and speckled with rust, which told me it was Dad's, pulled from the deep of the basement.

Jimmy started toward the steps.

Mom caught him by the arm. "No. Don't."

He twisted free and moved slowly downstairs. Mom followed. I looked behind me at my dark room and suddenly it seemed like the best place for a bad person to hide, so I got out of there.

The pop can was on the kitchen counter. Mom's back was against the wall with the phone in her hand. "I'm calling the cops."

"No." Jimmy checked behind the couch. "Not yet."

"The can isn't open," I said. Someone could have set it there and forgot. I picked up the can. "And it's warm."

Jimmy came toward me. His eyes were mean, like when I open his door without knocking. I backed away. He grabbed the can from my hand. "It's diet," he said. "Who drinks diet?"

I wanted to say Mom drinks diet, but I kept my mouth shut.

He pointed with the knife. "Next to Mom. Go."

The reason Jimmy acted so tough this morning was because of yesterday. Yesterday I went in the house and started homework right after school. I do that when I have the key. Soon as I got up to make a snack, the phone rang.

"Guess who this is," said a man.

"I don't know," I said.

"Just guess."

I thought hard. "I can't."

"I have a sore throat. My voice is different. That's why you don't know who it is."

I kept quiet.

"Now do you know who it is?"

"Mitch?"

He turned his face from the phone like he was talking to someone else. "Mitch?" he said. "No—not Mitch."

"I'm hanging up," I said.

"No. No, I'm just joking with you," he said. "It's Mitch."

"You don't sound like Mitch."

"Like I said, I have a sore throat." He laughed for no good reason, and then asked, "Do you ever get sick?"

I didn't answer. It was a stupid question.

"Because when I get sick I want to feel better." His breath was loud in my ear. "Can you do that for me, Dawn? Make me feel better?" His voice changed. He wasn't joking anymore. "I know how you can make me feel better, Dawn." He sucked in air through his teeth.

How did he know my name? He wasn't Mitch and he knew my name. I made tight fists and tried hard as I could not to cry.

I hung up the phone and backed into the corner and looked around the room.

The front blinds were open. I dropped to the floor and crawled. I tried not to cry, but everything was coming out when I breathed. I reached for the cord and pulled the blinds closed. What if he was outside watching me? He saw me close the blinds and knew where I was. I tried to stop crying and I tried not to scream, but I screamed and screamed.

"What's going on?" The stairs shook as Jimmy ran down.

"You're here?" I screamed.

"I came in the back," he yelled.

"He's coming to get me!" I screamed.

"Who?" he shouted.

"The man!"

"Quiet down!"

I screamed and screamed. "The man on the phone is coming to get me." I didn't want to cry in front of Jimmy. He needed to know I was tough. "He said he was Mitch, but he wasn't." I took a breath. "He said my name." A sob caught in my throat. "He knew my name."

Jimmy's face relaxed and I saw he wanted to hug me like when he was young. Then his eyes got mean. "It was him."

"No," I said. "It wasn't."

"He had something to do with this. Trust me." He pulled up the blinds and stared out the window and said, "I'm going to make him pay."

I wiped my eyes. "How?" My voice was flimsy. I hated the sound of it.

"Beat him senseless."

"Sure," I said.

He looked straight at me. "You don't think I could?"

"No."

"I was the enforcer in hockey," he said, quiet now. "You know what that means, right? It was my job to beat guys up. My *only* job."

I pushed a hand against the wall and stood. "Then go do your job."

I'm standing at my front door, searching the dim, waiting for Jimmy to answer from his room upstairs.

"Jimmy?" I say again, louder.

If he's home, he's in his room. After Dad died, Jimmy shut himself up in there, like if he stayed inside, he could make life stop. He could close the door and everything would stay like it was and never change and the bad stuff couldn't get in. But now I know—better than Jimmy, even—the bad stuff always finds a way.

Jimmy doesn't answer and now my body recognizes that a bathroom is close.

I step through the door, out of the cold. The heater starts, and a breeze of air flows through the vents. I climb the stairs still holding my pants and barely make it to the bathroom, but I do and the relief is like coming up for air after a long swim. Just before I walk into the hall, I stop myself and listen. I wait a few seconds, then move toward Jimmy's room. His door is almost shut, but not latched. I push it open, holding my breath.

He isn't here and I'm sure I'm alone, so I go to his closet and sit on the floor with my knees pulled in high. All I can think is that tomorrow I'll have to come in by myself again, wondering. Even if I have the key.

Directly in front of me is Jimmy's hockey stick. He stopped playing a couple years ago, right after Dad died. Just put his stick in the closet and never got it out again. I reach for it. It's bottom-heavy and weird to hold because the stick is square, not round, and all corners.

I step out of the closet and swing it, hitting an imaginary puck. The stick clips Jimmy's lamp and a chunk of ceramic lands on the nightstand with dust crumbles around it.

The stick rights itself in my hands, the toe always wants to point down. I stare at the gap in the lamp—and then I swing. I'm smashing the lamp to pieces and I can't stop. The lightbulb, the shade, the metal ring at the top. I'm breathing heavy, realizing what I've done and adding up how mad Jimmy's going to be at me, for being in his room alone, for breaking his lamp, for daring to pick up the stick, for being alive, because, really, that's what he's mad about, that we're all alive, especially him—when the door creaks open.

It's Mitch.

The blood pulses in my cheeks and suddenly my head feels like it might pull away from my body and float. I cannot pass out.

I push my back into the corner and hold the stick as tight as I can. I check the window and calculate how fast I can get it open and jump out.

"Dawn," he says. "I want—" He's searching for the right words. "I'm here to apologize." He moves a step toward me. His face is a mess of bruises and cuts.

"Don't come any closer." I lift the stick so I can swing it like a bat.

"A buddy of mine—not even a good buddy, just a guy I know really—thought it'd be funny to call and mess with you," says Mitch. "Last night he told me what he did and I—" He lifts his hand. It's taped and two fingers are puffy and purple.

Yesterday after the phone call, after Jimmy and I had stopped yelling at each other, he left the front room and I followed him. He grabbed his keys.

"You're not leaving me here alone," I said.

He looked at me, picked up the phone, and dialed. "Hey. Is your sister home?" He listened. "I'll be over in a few minutes with Dawn. You gotta help me with something."

He took me over to his friend Pete's house and left me with Pete's sister, Molly. We watched TV on their couch without talking till Jimmy and Pete came home, energy popping off them. Jimmy's knuckles were scraped up and bloody. Pete kept sniffing his nose, like he'd suddenly developed a cold, but I saw dried blood in one of the nostrils. On the drive home, I asked Jimmy where he went.

"None of your business," he said.

"How did you get in?" I ask Mitch.

"The door was open," he says. "I knocked, but no one answered."

We stare at each other. I haven't moved an inch.

He lifts his hands and says, "That's all I wanted to say." One hand is bandaged and the other is holding something with the last three fingers. He takes a step back like he's surrendering or something and Jimmy comes up behind him and gets him in a chokehold. He grabs for Jimmy's arm, but Jimmy isn't going to let go this time and he's pulling Mitch backwards towards the ground. Mitch's eyes close and he slumps. Jimmy lets him drop.

"Is he dead?" I ask, panicked.

"No, just passed out."

Jimmy looks like he used to before Dad and everything else— boy eyes and a standstill jaw that's quit the constant flexing. I'm sure he's going to hug me, and it makes me happy that my brother is back, the one who used to play games with me, the one I used to watch cartoons with on Saturday mornings, just the two of us, quiet, eating cereal. I'm proud that I know my brother better than anyone else.

"Give me the stick," he says.

"Why?" My breath is coming fast. I'm scared of what he's going to do. "He said he didn't do it. He said he beat up his friend, that's why his hand is like that."

"Don't be stupid, Dawn," he says. "Give me the stick."

"No," I say. "Just drag him down the steps and leave him outside. Or throw him out the window."

Jimmy bends down and picks up something from the carpet next to Mitch's hand. He comes toward me holding it straight out in front of him until it's practically on my nose.

The key.

I remember now. Yesterday. I put the spare back under the rock before I went inside.

"He's a liar, Dawn," says Jimmy. "I beat the shit out of him last night. And he came back here for revenge—on me—by messing with you."

Outside the snow is falling big, like the ground is pulling it down faster than it wants to drop. The night Dad died, the night of the car accident with Jimmy, it was snowing. Slower, though. Icy. Mom and I left Dad to wait for Jimmy after his game. How many times have I wished we'd switched cars? If Dad had taken me home instead of Jimmy, he'd still be alive. Or maybe I should have stayed at the rink with Jimmy. Of course, it never would have happened like that. Mom and me, Jimmy and Dad. There wasn't any other way.

I blink and Jimmy comes into focus. "Maybe you shouldn't do this," I say. But we both know it can't be stopped.

"You should go," he says.

I expect Jimmy to snatch the stick out of my hands, let his anger burn red on my skin, but he lifts it so easy and light, like we're on the moon and nothing has any weight.

# Waiver

A GUARD hands me a box with the clothes Mom brought for me to wear out of here, and I don't know if she realizes—they're the same ones I wore in. If I didn't have to touch them, I wouldn't. I'd toss the box on a wild bonfire and walk away.

Outside, there's warm sunshine instead of cold fluorescent prison light. A breeze. The air smells like a dandelion ready for a wish. A dry kiss of wind moves like soft lips across my cheek.

My mom falls into me, wraps her arm around the back of my neck, and pulls me toward her by the crook of her elbow.

"Jimmy" is all she can say.

Her tears wet the skin of my collarbone. Behind her is my little sister, Dawn, with her tight shirt announcing she's a teenager now. A sharp pain twists at my ribs and I realize what I should have known all along: I can't protect her.

Mom drives and we're in our regular places: I'm in the passenger seat and Dawn's in the back so the two of us can trade looks whenever Mom says something annoying. But no one talks. What's there to discuss? How I wrecked my own life just to prove what a tough guy I was? At least I had the sense not to kill that loser. At least I stopped short of that.

We head into town and kids are outside on their bikes, a woman walks into the grocery store, the mailman reaches an arm out of his truck and opens a mailbox and what the hell is going on? I feel like I'm on the set of a movie, like it's all been staged so I can pretend the last two years never happened.

We get out of the car at home and Mom and Dawn move so careful, I have the urge to shout. But I push it down because I'll scare them. They'll wonder if I'm dangerous now and it's good for them to wonder because I'm not sure myself.

They let me go in the house first, polite, like I'm a guest. Because I am.

Nothing's changed—the furniture's in the same spots, Mom's figurines are up on the shelf in the same order they've always been, my room's like it was, except straightened. That's what fucks you up in the end. Everything's as you left it and no one's changed. Except you. You're the one who's different. And because you aren't who you used to be, who they want you to be, you don't fit anymore.

Even my own bed seems dented for a stranger's body. I can't sleep— might as well get dressed. Inside the toe of a basketball shoe I've never worn is a fold of twenties. I turn the shoe in my palms and trace the stitching with my thumbnail, then pull out the money. My clothes from yesterday sit clean and cool in the dryer. I put them on and push my heels into the stiff shoes.

I take a small stack of the money for myself and leave the rest on the kitchen table. I write a note—"See you when I get back"— and ease out of the house.

I'm in the driver's seat of my car and it's the first time I'm my full self. Old and new. I'm not out of place because the car's mine and I can be who I choose. The engine takes a second to catch, but the car starts. If I could give it a hug, I would. Slap it on the shoulder and ask, "How've you been, old buddy?"

I jump at the sound of a knock on the window. Dawn.

"You just got here and you're leaving?" She's upset, but won't let herself cry. "Where are you going?"

"For a drive."

"Where?"

"I don't know, Dawn. Just around."

"Why'd you leave money on the table, then, with that note?"

I sigh, cut the engine.

"You just got home. We need you here."

"No, you don't, Dawn. You're better off without me. There's nothing but trouble hanging around the edges here and I'll just bring it into the house."

"So you want to go find trouble somewhere else? Mom can't take it."

"Mom can take it."

"What about me? Don't you care about me?"

"I do. That's why I'm leaving."

"Some logic. You *suck*. All you think about is you."

Now she's got me near tears because I don't want to let her down. "I know you want me to stay, but I can't, Dawn. I just can't."

"Fine. Leave. I don't fucking care." She runs to the house and flips me the bird before she goes inside.

Town's still waking up as I drive the empty streets. Of course, the gas station's open and McDonald's. I pull into the Walmart lot and sit there until a blue smock opens the front doors. I head in, straight to the jewelry counter and find the best watch I can buy with the cash I have. Brown leather band, silver face with a ring on top that turns, notched for every second. I tell the woman at the counter not to bother giving me the box.

The office is in a strip mall with *For Lease* signs stuck in dirty windows on either side. I go through the glass door and stand there, not sure what to do, so I study the posters hung straight and perfect on the walls, like they'll give me the answer to any question I ask.

A guy comes through the door from the back. He approaches me, hand offered. We shake.

"Staff Sergeant Carroll," he says.

"James Kepner," I say.

"What can I do for you, James?"

"I want to enlist."

"Happy to hear it." He leads me to a desk and we sit. "Let me tell you about all the benefits, incentives, and bonuses, not to mention the pride and honor that comes with being a member of the United States military."

"Sure," I say.

There's a video made specifically to get my testosterone pumping, which it does. He shows me some brochures—the whole sales pitch, which isn't necessary. I'm in.

"So, still interested?"

"Yes, I am."

He moves the mouse of his computer and the fan starts. "Very good. You're eighteen?"

"Be nineteen in a few months."

"Let's get started then." He asks me my full name, birth date, address—all that. Then, "Have you ever been convicted of a felony?"

"Yes."

He leans away from the keyboard. "That's a problem."

"I heard there's a waiver."

He slides back from the computer and sets his hands on his thighs, elbows out. No point typing any more. "Only in rare cases. Nonviolent crimes."

My leg has a mind of its own and starts to bounce. I put a hand on my knee to stop it. "You're in the middle of two wars and, from what I hear, you're in bad need of soldiers."

"Not so bad we're going to start using felons." He's wearing a watch. All metal. "The Army won't issue a waiver." He stands. "Thanks for coming in."

I wait, but he doesn't flinch. "My guess is you've seen my kind before. The kind who has no clue what's ahead. Because if I did have a clue, I wouldn't be here. But the thing is, I know exactly what's coming for me. I want what's coming."

"And what is that?"

My dad didn't want me playing sports. Which made it all the worse—that I was such a good hockey player. "Sports get in the way of grades," he said. "I want you to get an education, work in an air-conditioned office. Use your brain, not your hands." Every once in a while, he'd complain about having to come straight from his shift to my match and wouldn't he just love to have a hot dinner at home instead of potato chips and pop from the concession stand? But I knew he only meant it a little.

Last game of the playoffs, I was surprised he showed up. He'd been working swing shifts and it'd been his last night shift. I saw him outside the rink as they were announcing our names and I held up my hands, asking what was he doing there. He waved me off, telling me not to worry about it, he was there.

On the drive home after we won, he told me he'd switched shifts with his friend, so he could watch the game. I damn near cried, happy we won, happy to be with my dad. Mom and Dawn rode home separate because he'd come right from work.

We were waiting at a red light and he clapped a hand on my shoulder and squeezed and I thought he was going to say "Good job, son" or "I'm proud of you," but what he said was "I guess hockey ain't so bad."

We looked at each other and sniffed the same laugh then the car shattered. The dashboard and the windshield were coming to crush me. My knees rammed up against the dash and my head hit so hard my teeth slammed shut. I had a sense that I screamed, but I can't remember the sound of it. Just that my mouth was open and something was coming out. I know it was open because later I pulled glass out of the soft part of my cheek.

When the noise stopped and I opened my eyes, my dad wasn't in his seat. The windshield was gone. The cargo van that'd hit us was upside down in the median, wheels spinning. My hands had glass in them and I was spitting out shards and my knees were up near my chest, but I unfastened my seat belt and found a way to stand on my shaky legs. I searched the dark for my dad and saw him lying on the cement, facedown.

I went over to him and his face was all blood, but his eyes were open and his breaths were fast.

"Dad?" I said, kneeling next to him.

He just stared.

I was afraid to move him. I got down so he could see me. His eyes were blank, like he was already miles away from his own body.

"Dad."

He looked straight at me and focused.

The thing is: he was breathing—really fast. Like, *huh huh huh.* Then he wasn't.

"One thing the past two years has taught me, sir, is that in order to survive a place like prison or a battlefield, you got to be outside your own body. There's you and there's your body. And if I'm the guy who gets smoked, at least I'll be my whole self for one last split second."

I don't care anymore about what Carroll's going to do. I don't care about prison, or what comes next, the military, the war, this office—anything, really. All I care about is that, right now, at this moment, someone is listening to what I have to say. And if Carroll's the only one who hears me, so be it.

"Maybe that's what we're all driving toward and we just don't realize. One split second of pure truth at the very end."

He crosses his arms. I'm making him uncomfortable or impatient. Or both. "And you think this—perspective—on life will make you a good solider?"

"No," I say. "What'll make me a good soldier is that I take the hits in order to win." I start thinking about hockey and my dad and my throat gets tight.

"So, you're ready to die then?" he says. "Because that could be the outcome, you realize."

"We're all going to die, sir."

"What if you don't die? What if you end up with no legs?"

I lift my hands. "What if I come back in tact? Just my mind's gone," I say. "Then I'll be where I am right now."

This is a new one for Carroll. I can see I've thrown him for a loop. He's stuck in place—can't go forward, can't drop back. He'll have to vouch for me, jump through hoops, form after form, phone calls, face to face. Will I be worth the fight?

"What's your name again?" he asks.

"James," I say. "But my friends call me Jimmy."

He exhales, rubs a finger across his bottom lip. "Jimmy," he says, half there, like he's talking to himself. I can see he wants to usher me to the door—get back to his bagel and coffee—that he doesn't want to bet on this problem hand I've dealt him, wishes I was already a forgotten memory.

But then, he pulls a sheet of paper from the desk and says, "We have to start over." He uncaps a pen. "Last name?"

# As I Lay Living

WE HAVE been living the stories of men for centuries. One story men tell is that a woman isn't a woman until she is ripped open by the body of another. A woman's power, men assert, can only be found in the secret spaces of her body. The longer she keeps a secret, the more power she holds. As soon as she exposes her secret, her power dims.

My mother knew better. She moved in the world of men and discovered their secret, that power comes from outside the body. *Money*, she said, *is power. Never give up your money. When you have children—if you have children—never stop working. Work, work, work, work, work.* I was a child myself when she told me this, but that word, *work*, burrowed into my chest, down into my gut and never left me.

What I learned on my own, separate from my mother, yet through my work, was that death has its own power and anything else is just an approximation of it. We may exert our control over life, but death controls us. I am under its control now. It has showed me that my mother and men have been selling delusions. That what men really want control of isn't life, but death.

Women create life in their secret spaces of power. Men want to control death—who has the power to kill (men and men only), how, and when.

My son went to war. He was daring death. *Come and get me*, he taunted. I should have known why. It's obvious now, but then—I was too tied up in work. My own work, nursing, is women's attempt at pushing death away from people. But we nurses often lose to death. Maybe more than soldiers. We know death is wild and unpredictable and cannot be trusted.

Jimmy fooled Dawn and me. We thought he saw war as a path of lava he had to walk across to remake himself whole. Burn out the rot of deep wounds so that new skin could form. Instead, he just covered the wounds. At first when he sent us pictures, he looked like he'd aged backwards. With all his hair gone, his eyes seemed larger, like the scared boy who watched his father die. Those eyes had narrowed with every passing year until I couldn't remember their exact color. Imagine not knowing in great detail your own son's eyes.

But as time marched forward, the photos of his appearance ricocheted off the scared boy picture and flew in the opposite direction. His hair grew, a beard covered his mouth, then later his neck. His clothes flowed off of him until I no longer trusted that the pictures were of my son. He looked like one of the men he was sent across the world to kill. We had already adjusted to his new self once, after being locked away for years. How would we adapt again? Each time he left and returned, we, too, had to leave who we were behind and step back into someone old, who we were before. When he came home, he didn't want to know that we were new, too, that time drew us closer to death. He wanted to show us his difference, that he now lived in the realm of men, and yet he wanted us to stay the same. He didn't want to know Dawn believed men's stories about her secrets, how they'd gained power over her—something else beyond his control. So he left.

Dawn swallowed the men's stories and let them break her apart. She believed them when they said her only power lay in her body. She came to me, satisfied, despite falling for their lies. She had created a life.

I slapped her. How could she be fooled so easily? And then I threatened her. All her father's death money we'd set aside for her education? Gone. Unless she realized her ultimate power, the power men want solely for themselves—the power to kill.

Dawn knew I was right, that she'd consumed a lie whole and it lived inside her. It was my fault, in the end, that I'd allowed her to be easily tricked. She rid herself of it, then cut off all her hair—big eyes, aging backwards. I'd seen it before. Jimmy.

She went to college and grew her hair. Again, long, until it covered her face, until she was nearly drowning in it. Then she cut it and carried on, as all women do. We carry on. She decided her work would be in helping children speak, smooth out their words, not skip around or stop completely.

Men and their weak pronunciations. They sell us empty promises like, *Women and children first.*

Yes, first, I say. To die.

Which is worse: to not know how your child died or to know in great detail, second by agonizing second, what happened?

Men kill women where we are being educated because the power of education is one of the secrets they don't want us to discover. My daughter died protecting other people's children. A teenage boy aimed his rage through a classroom window. A bullet smashed apart my daughter's jaw and tunneled through her brain. Three more bullets exploded her insides, but, if I am allowed one hope, it's that the first bullet brought forth the power of death.

Funerals are for the living, not the dead, and, the moment my daughter died, I lay down in my bed and refused to leave. I'd helped the living fight death my entire adult life, and I'd lost, again. I no longer had a sense of reality. Did my son lift me out of bed, dress me, comb my hair, push shoes onto my feet, and bring me to her funeral? Or did I dream that?

By my mother's definition and by men's, I am now without power. I spend my days between reality and sleep. Is there anywhere else to live for a mother whose children are dead or lost? If my mother were here, I would ask her. What do you say now, Mother? Where is my power? Is it a mirage that disappears when we get close? I have lived longer than her. I suspect I hold more wisdom than she ever did. One truth she taught me as her life was ending is that death is a mercy. A relief. Living is the terrible thing.

Maybe men were right. Women's power does lie in our bodies, except not where they claim. Our power is in our mind. Because I have my own definition of power. Power lies in dreams. Dreams are just desires, of the body, the mind, played out with the people we love. And hate. What happens to a mother whose desires vanish? A woman with no one to love? What will she dream of? I'm alone in one world—reality—but to be without dreams, alone there, too? Tell me, Mother. Keep me company. Help me find our power, together in one mind. Wait until I'm asleep.

# A Month of Summer

*In the life of each of us ... there is a place remote and islanded, and given to endless regret or secret happiness.*

—Sarah Orne Jewett, *The Country of the Pointed Firs*

ONCE, BETWEEN the stage of life when time moves slowly, like a child's school day in winter, and the stage when time leapfrogs overhead, I sat atop a gray-and-white dappled horse in a city neighborhood surrounded by narrow homes with slick-tiled roofs and flower boxes offering blooms in all the colors of joy. The perfume of flowers mixed with that of coffee and the sweet yeast of bread left to cool on a sill. Cyclists sped past, their wire baskets cradling mesh bags of apples, loaves of pumpernickel wrapped in parchment, marzipan. A cyclist's bell chimed, triple-sectioned: the windup press of the thumb, the peak, the reverb of return. A sweat drip traveled a winding path down my jaw and dropped a long mark onto my shirt, already soaked through in the back. The horse swished her tail and pushed a hoof forward, rocking me to one side.

*Pay attention.*

Her careful reminder.

I've been in the opera world long enough to be well aware that we singers are considered egomaniacs. I'm a little different than the rest. Life has served me up a heavy dose of reality, so I'm one of the few performers who considers any amount of time on stage to be a gift. I am what the professional opera singers call a hobbyist—I only sing in the chorus, never the named roles.

Until now.

In one hour, on the verge of my fortieth birthday, I will perform the role of Kanna in Schubert's *Sakontala* on my home stage with the Florida Grand Opera. I should be nervous. Shaking. But I'm not. I have practiced every free minute of every day since I won the part. This role might be the door that opens just wide enough to walk through. Or it could be my only chance, my one time to shine.

And, if that's the case, I'm okay with it. I'm calm because I have nothing to lose. No matter what happens, I am one of the few lucky souls who can step into the light of an opera stage and know its warmth.

One snowy day during high school, my German teacher, Frau Williams, approached me in the hallway between classes to ask if I would be interested in a year abroad. I sputtered a response about how it sounded out-of-this-world awesome, but I doubted I'd be able to go.

"Think about it," she said. "A year abroad would be good for you." We both knew what she meant. Being different in a small town was a job. Frau was different—her curly hair, always alight with static, framed her face like fur edging a hood. A year prior she'd started a theater troupe with a few brave souls. She drove an old Japanese car. The Japanese car alone—

"But I'd miss an entire year of band." I wanted to study music after high school. A year off could have very real consequences.

"I'm sure you can arrange lessons." She patted me on the shoulder and left. Frau was always in a hurry.

When I told Mom, she didn't say anything at first. Then, after a few moments, she said, "An entire year?"

"A school year—technically, ten months."

"And, how much?"

"Nothing beyond spending money," I said. "There's a scholarship for kids who can't afford the fees."

She thought about it, then said, "Let's see what your grandpa thinks."

A few days later I was practicing my bassoon in the kitchen when Mom came in.

"I heard the tail end," she said, rubbing her forehead. "It was very good."

"Why are you home?"

"I think I'm coming down with the flu," she said.

I packed up my bassoon and took it, along with my music stand, to my room. When I came back, she was lying on the couch with the orange crocheted afghan over her.

"Do you want some water?"

"Ginger ale might be better," she said.

I poured her a glass in the kitchen and brought it to her.

She took a few sips and offered the glass back to me. "You should go to Germany." She rolled over, pulling the blanket tight around her shoulders.

I waited until Chore Day—Saturday to everyone else—to talk to Grandpa. We were cleaning out the back gutter and I was on the ladder, which I hated. Every move I made, creak. Grandpa had all day and worked slow because he could. I just wanted to get the cleaning over with, so I grabbed by the handful and he complained I was doing a sloppy job.

"Now, dammit, listen when I tell you. Whether it's playing the horn or clearing leaves," he said. "Do it right."

We were almost finished by the time I got the courage to speak. I said my piece about going to Germany and he kept working, pulling a thick twig from the downspout. After a while, I figured his silence was a no and started to climb down.

"Why Germany?" he asked.

I steadied myself on the ladder. "Because the high school offers two languages—French and German—and I picked German." I stepped to the ground, took his full trash bag, and handed him a new one. "Besides," I said, "this whole area of Ohio was drained and cleared by the Germans. We're all just a bunch of Krauts anyway."

"We're no Krauts, son." He paused to catch his breath, leaning his forearm on the gutter.

I moved the ladder a few feet away and made my way up.

"I saw." He stared at me until I looked him in the eyes. "Germans are a cruel people. Especially to those who don't fit." He stepped down a rung. "Like you."

My host family met me in the waiting area of my arrival gate at the Frankfurt Airport. Helmut, my host father, held a sign with my name scrawled in slanted German cursive. The mother, Dagmar, pulled a small German flag through her fingers, and their son, Lars, waved a piece of graph paper weighed down by a hand-drawn American flag. I tugged at the hem of my shirt, approached them, and said hello. Lars had his mother's curly hair and his father's ruddy cheeks, his father's easy smile and, as I would soon learn, his mother's plain adherence to truth. He was nine, all boy, and wore it under his fingernails.

Being placed with a family in Heidelberg was like winning the exchange-student lottery. Heidelberg is an old city wedged in the valley of a river, the Neckar, surrounded by hills. Main Street is a cobblestone road that leads pedestrians past centuries-old buildings. Streetcars clang through the middle of the busy streets, and at night Heidelberg's castle glows atop a high hill. On the hill that faces the castle, Mark Twain was rumored to have written Huckleberry Finn. Heidelberg, after all, is derived from a word that translates to Huckleberry Mountain.

Helmut drove through the city, then parked at the bottom of the path opposite the castle, the *Philosophenweg*, and we began to hike up the narrow cement walk. Almost immediately it became steep and required huge reaching steps with every stride. We paused at the top of the first crest and I wiped sweat from my brow with the inside of my elbow. They found a cement table and sat.

*What do you think of the view?* asked Helmut.

I cleared sweat from my eyes with the hem of my T-shirt. *Super*, I said, slumped on the bench, panting.

The Trägers looked at each other.

*Okay, then*, said Dagmar. *Now we go home.*

Their house was bright in the right places—the entrance, the kitchen—while also perfectly shaded for a nap in others—the family room, the bedrooms. The open windows moved fresh air room to room, picking up hints of tea, grass, and laundry soap to make their home's unique scent, something every home has, like a homing beacon for the family who lives within to carry while they're away. I wouldn't understand until many years later that a home isn't made of walls, framed prints, and armchairs. A home becomes another member of the family that inhabits it, absorbing their personalities to form one of its own.

On that day, I believed Dagmar had baked a plum cake especially for me. Soon after, I came to realize she baked a pastry every other day for *Mittagspause*, our midday break. She spooned tea into a double-pot coffee maker, one pot for coffee, one for tea, then Lars ran me around the house. He skipped sideways through the hall, speaking in a continuous chain of German, none of which I understood at the time, though now I inexplicably remember.

*What is your school like? Do you watch television? I hear Americans watch a lot of television. Here's your room. Do you like it? There's a TV for you.*

I hurried after him down the stairs best I could. He flung open the kitchen door and I followed, moments behind.

Helmut looked up from his newspaper, amused by the pair of us. *It's going to be a loud year.* Then, to Dagmar, *Two boys. Are you ready?*

Bitte schön, she said, dragging out the *o. You mean three boys.* She held up her thumb and first two fingers.

*Remember,* said Helmut to Dagmar. *I'm no boy.* They raised their eyebrows at each other, amused, daring the other to speak. Helmut folded his paper. Lars started pulling plates from the cabinet.

*I—change.* I lifted my damp shirt with my fingertips.

Ja, ja, said Dagmar. *We'll wait for you.* Dagmar's lips were shaped by the frequent pronunciation of *ü,* like someone who'd just finished playing the trumpet.

Dagmar had laid a washcloth and towel on the low foam couch that unfolded into my bed for the coming year. I took a quick shower, not quite sure which bottle was shampoo, which was soap or conditioner, but figured I'd be clean no matter what, so I rushed through and went back to the kitchen. As soon as I sat, they began to eat.

Dagmar pulled an upside-down spoon of cream from between her lips. *Does the cake taste good?*

The plum cake was sweet and tart, but not so much it hurt the back of my jaw. *The cake is number one*, I said. *From everything.*

She nodded, satisfied I realized what she already knew.

*After this, Yulli*, said Lars. *We'll go across the street to the stalls and take Blume for a trot.*

*What?* I said.

*Yulli*, said Lars. *You don't say "What." You say "How, please?"*

*Okay. How, please?*

He stood from the table, too full of energy to sit. *My horse, Blume, needs exercise. We have a stall across the street and a fenced in pasture.*

*I don't understand*, I said. How could a horse be across the street in the middle of the city?

*Come on*, he said. *Have you ever been on a horse?*

*I not go horse*, I said. *Tired. I don't know how. I never go horse. And I am heavy.*

*Blume can handle you*, Lars said. *But, yes, you are quite fat.*

I couldn't help but laugh. Here was the truth, proud of itself, unapologetic. My affection for Lars was already the kind a wisp-furred teddy bear might feel for the boy who kept him vised tight to his side.

*Okay*, I said. *I'll try.*

Super geil! Lars raised his arms, accidentally flinging his spoon, full of cream, at the wall.

Dagmar sighed. *You have to learn to control yourself, Lars.*

*Make sure you clean that up*, said Helmut.

*I help*, I said. The way it worked, I cleaned the wall while Lars talked.

*My dad rides Blume all the time. Blume will teach you what to do. She's a good horse. You'll see. Do you go to lots of rodeos back home?*

And on and on.

After a week with the Trägers, my novelty wore off and we settled into the routine of life, which was a relief. Being the center of attention is fun and exciting—and exhausting.

*Yulli, follow me*, said Helmut. *Let's fix Dagmar's bike chain.* Helmut wore purple glasses, tight red jeans, and green socks with sandals. I couldn't figure out how it all went together, but it suited him. *Look here*, he said when we reached his workbench in the garage. He showed me the chain, wiping the grease away with his thumb. *The link broke. Good thing she was almost home when it happened.*

I stared at the small prongs bent wide. *Only one link?*

*Defective*, he said.

Helmut pulled open the tiniest wooden drawer with a knob the size of a pea. *When repairing a chain you must replace two links, not one. The links are paired.*

*Why not just buy a new chain?*

*The back cassette wears at the same rate as the chain. When you put a new chain on, it isn't worn the same as the sprockets in the back. They don't work together as well as with the old one.* His fingers had already begun to turn black from the grease. It was strange to see him with dirty hands. *What are you going to study at the Uni?*

*Music.*

He pulled the loose chain across the counter. *The bassoon?*

*I think so.* I'd practiced a few times since arriving, but not nearly enough.

*Then you must have lessons while you're here.* He pointed at a small tool with a handle and metal bar that spun. *Pass me the chain tool.*

*My grandfather thinks I should study something more practical.*

*You could do both. Music and business. Or music and teaching.* His tone signaled that he didn't believe what he was saying to be very groundbreaking or important, but until then, no one had ever told me I had options, that I could make my own path and didn't have to follow the one set before me, treaded down by so many feet.

*Your grandfather is right—you must be able to pay your bills. You can't eat musical notes. On the other hand, don't deny yourself joy.* He threaded the chain into the tool's channel and turned the metal bar. He met some resistance and shook with the effort. *Don't push the pin all the way out. You'll never get it back in.* He put the new links in and pushed one of the pins. *After the chain's on the bike—the other pin.*

The door leading to the kitchen opened and slammed. *What are you doing out here?* Lars wedged himself between us.

*Fixing your mother's bike chain.*

*I want to help.*

Helmut kneeled next to the bike. *Hold this steady while I put on the chain*, he said.

Both Lars and I reached for the seat. I pulled my hand back and let him hold it. *I should probably do my homework*, I said.

Lars watched his father work.

*Bye.*

I thought they might tell me to stay, but they were already caught up in their own conversation.

I met with my new music teacher, Herr Keller, after *Gymnasium*. At first, lessons were twice a week, then I trudged up to the attic room nearly every weekday. The musty, windowless room smelled of sweat, spit, and wet wood. Lessons became something I dreaded. Herr Keller refused to speak German and only criticized me. Never encouraged. But I knew, somehow, the criticism meant he believed I was worth the effort. I'd heard him with other students as I waited for my lesson to begin and, to them, he spoke in surprisingly hushed German. Those students were his bread and butter. With me, he was forever impatient. Looking back, I understand—because now I'm the instructor—that every teacher is searching for his prodigy. The low pay, the long hours, the squandered personal time—they must all amount to something. And that something is a prodigy the teacher can point to and say, *I did that.* The student understands this from deep within and feels an obligation to achieve success and pushes and fights to reach this goal for both of them. If the student doesn't feel this obligation, then he is not the prodigy and the teacher must find another.

Herr Keller scheduled extra lessons the Trägers didn't pay for. I knew because I brought them the bill every month.

Once I could not get the pitch right. The notes kept breaking. The bassoon plays almost like a bagpipe, except the notes are supposed to be steady, not wavering.

Herr Keller stopped me and put away the music. I knew this meant he had reached the end of his tolerance. He rubbed his temple with his right hand, which was missing half an index finger. One day, I hoped to find the courage to ask what happened.

"If you desire to play zeh bassoon," he said, "ziss is a difficult instrument, *ga*? When it is false, the sound is terrible. Only when zeh player has it perfect"—he dropped a fist in his palm—"beauty."

"Yes."

"So why choose?"

"It fits me."

"No," said Herr Keller. "Zeh tuba fits."

"But the bassoon matches what's inside," I said.

Herr Keller folded his hands at his belly button. "You are wrong. On the inside you are a harp."

I exhaled, not sure of what to do. Start over with a new instrument? And where would I get a harp? It wasn't like I could strap it to the back of my bike. Then there was the money I'd need to lease one. And, really, harpists mainly ended up playing weddings and charity events.

*What do you in truth want?* asked Herr Keller.

*To go to school for music,* I said.

*No! This is not something a person wants. To go to school. Think, goddamn it. Think beyond school. What do you want?*

I was close to tears, but would rather be stabbed in the foot than cry in front of Herr Keller.

*Tell me. What do you want?*

I took a breath so my voice would be steady. *To sing.*

He pressed his mouth into a line and nodded once. *Good. Now we can quit wasting time—yours, but, more importantly, mine. As well as the Trägers' money.* He began packing his briefcase.

*The lesson's over?*

*I am not a voice instructor,* he said. *I will ask one of my friends, Frau Doktor Schmidt, at the Hochschule für Musik in Mannheim and see if she can take you on.*

*But,* I said. *You're my instructor.*

*Is your hearing defective? I don't teach voice.* He snapped his briefcase shut.

*I don't want another instructor.*

*It isn't about what you want,* he said. *It's about what you need.*

*Surely if you can teach instruments, you can teach voice. It's just another instrument.*

He set his briefcase on the music stand and paused to think. *You would be better off with a voice instructor.*

*I disagree.*

He lifted his briefcase from the stand. *You must learn from a teacher who understands pitch and tone. The exact*—he stabbed at the air with a flat hand, moving it lower with every word—*correct placement of each note.*

*You understand that*, I said.

He knocked twice on his head. *I didn't realize you had such a thick skull.*

*It's about as thick as yours.* Somehow I did it, after many months of challenges and disagreements. I finally made him laugh.

*Tomorrow, then*, he said.

*Tomorrow.*

Life in Heidelberg was a happy adjustment. School ended daily at two, at which time we students merged into the flow of bikes pedaling homeward or toward café tables for *Mittagspause.* Every now and then, Helmut or Dagmar had a work meeting and couldn't make it home in time, so Lars and I met and parked our bikes near the city center. We walked the shops eating a gyro or pizza or some type of humongous sausage with a roll on the side. Or we went to the Penny Markt for a snack and stood in the long line as white-haired ladies who'd earned their right to pass moved to the front in a slow drip. The cashier shouted out the total due in a monotone voice with his hand held close to my nose waiting for the money.

A few times, we went to a *Konditerei*, my personal version of heaven, with chocolate pastries of all flavors—hazelnut, orange, passion fruit, almond, pistachio. Once we crossed the bridge and spent an hour on the swing set close to the banks of the Neckar. I'd never felt so much like a kid than in that hour, stretching my legs toward sky, weightless for a moment.

At school, kids ate lunch in groups outside. I was a curiosity—a real, live American who understood them and spoke their language instead of one who asked in English for directions or to have his picture taken. As far as I could tell, if I'd've stepped out of the TV right in front of them, they'd have nodded once, as if to say, *That's what we figured.* But their interest in me waned when they realized I wasn't all that different from them.

Karsten and I moved closer to each other every day at break until eventually we sat side by side, me eating sliced eggs, him eating cucumbers, both on buttered pumpernickel. His appearance was strange to me at first. With his dark hair cropped close on the sides and bouncy on top and his collared Polo shirts straining against arm muscles, he looked American. Not to mention he was freshly showered every day. Certainly out of place among the slim-muscled, messy-haired German boys who showered twice a week. Karsten wanted to speak English. I didn't, but spoke just enough to keep him talking.

"Does Heidelberg please you?" he asked.

"Yes," I said. "Very much."

"And the school? Does the school please you?"

"It's difficult for me," I said. "My German is not good enough to be studying chemistry or geometry in another language, but my host father helps me."

"If you prefer, I may also help." He ate his sandwich in big bites, then took his time chewing. His jaw muscles flexed with each new attack.

He was beautiful. I wanted to tell him, but I knew better.

*Sakontala* is an opera about an Indian king who happens upon a hermitage in the woods as he's leading an army in slaying beasts. He meets a beautiful woman, Shakuntala, daughter of a holy sage, Kanna. The king is confused as to how she can be the daughter of a holy man, and she tells him she is, in fact, the daughter of a nymph, deserted at birth and cared for by birds until found and raised by the holy Kanna. The king, Dushyanta, promises to make her queen and care for their heir if she marries him on that day. They marry, consecrate the marriage, and he leaves with promises to send an army for her. She bears a son who has magical powers over savage beasts. After years of waiting for the army to arrive, Kanna urges Sakontala to journey to the king. As she stands before the king and asks that their son be crowned prince, the king denies both Sakontala and their son and orders her to leave. Devastated by the betrayal, she urges him to keep his promise. As she begins to walk away, the gods speak, confirming Sakontala's account as truth. The king then accepts his wife and son, claiming that, without the words of the gods, the veracity of their son would have been doubted throughout the kingdom.

*Sakontala* was a controversial choice for the Florida Grand Opera because Schubert left the opera unfinished and the completed version by Rasmussen wasn't well received. "An experiment without consequence," one reviewer said of the Saarbrücken production. Another, "an overloading of exotic stuff." But FGO's director wanted an opera entirely new to American audiences, if only for the right to say so. Plus, the criticism centered mainly on the stage direction. Our director believes he has an opportunity to make a name for himself as someone who finds little-known operas and spins them into gold.

Dagmar told me we were going on a trip to the North Sea and that I needed to pack a pair of shoes I didn't mind throwing away. Since I didn't have any shoes to spare, I brought my tennis shoes and hoped for the best. Helmut hooked a tiny trailer to the diesel-engine Mercedes and off we went. I never knew a car could cook at

160 kph with a trailer attached. I death-gripped the door handle with both hands and sighed relief when we exited to a two-lane road. After a few kilometers Helmut moved the car far to the right. The cars, semis, and busses coming at us in the opposite direction moved to their edge and a car behind us drove through the middle. I shut my eyes and crossed myself when it was over. Then a few minutes later, same thing.

We finally arrived at the campground. Helmut backed the trailer into a spot, turning the steering wheel one-handed and parking it exactly straight on the first try. He was that kind of driver—like he was born with perfect driving ability. We all unloaded the trunk while Helmut unhitched the trailer.

Dagmar checked her watch. *The ferry leaves in forty minutes.* Then, to me, *Are those the shoes you can throw away?*

I looked down at my black Oxfords and tugged the hem of my shirt. *No.* I sat on the picnic bench, changed into my tennis shoes and hurried into the car.

On the boat, I had to stay up top in the open air. When I sat downstairs with the Trägers, I got seasick. Every so often Lars came up to check on me.

*Yulli, come sit with us*, he shouted. *We're having a snack.*

*I can't. I'll get sick.* I stood in the back by the German flag snapping in the wind. I loved the sound.

He brought his sandwich and Fanta upstairs along with mine and we sat in deck chairs eating open-faced butter and roast beef sandwiches.

It was a quick ride. We arrived at a little island and docked. We walked in shops looking at tchotchkes and T-shirts, then sat and ate a bit more: quark, my favorite, like a mix of yogurt and whipped cream, cookies shaped like rolled newspaper with one end dipped in chocolate, tart cheese pressed with two fingers to a swatch of bread and eaten with our back teeth. Helmut offered me a piece of dried meat.

*Beef?* I asked.

*Eel,* he said.

Bleh. *No, thank you.*

*Come on, Yulli. One bite.* Lars ripped off a huge chunk and chewed.

I shook my head no.

Dagmar started collecting napkins and empty containers to throw away.

*Can I take a picture?* For once, I'd remembered my camera.

Helmut stood. *You sit. I'll take it.*

*No, please,* I said. *First you.*

I took three pictures of them, then Helmut waved down a passing tourist who took a picture of the four of us.

We sat for a while longer, then packed the leftovers and made our way back to the dock. The boat was gone. So was the water, replaced by a vast expanse of mud. We joined a group of people waiting, then a short, stocky woman walked up and called us all to attention.

*Now we begin our return,* she said. *At some points we will walk through the water, maybe up to our knees. But most of the journey we will be in the mud.*

I looked at Dagmar. *Walk?*

*Yes, Yulli,* she said. *We walk back.*

*The whole way?*

She laughed. *The whole way.*

*How long does it take?*

*Oh, not long. Five hours.*

My mouth dropped.

Lars said, *Yulli. It's going to be* super geil. *We'll see crabs and worms. Sometimes you get stuck in the mud and we have to pull you out. Sometimes the mud takes your shoes and won't give them back.*

And it happened just as he said. Worm trails like miniature serpent mounds in the mud. Lars pulling at my wrists when I got sucked into a mud sinkhole, which let me keep my shoes. The crabs posturing with their claws. The tan, hairy-legged guide caught one and held it up.

*You see?* she said. *A male crab has two penises.* She pointed to one like a curved awl, then the other.

When we finished, we laughed at ourselves, legs stiff with dried mud. I pulled off my ruined shoes, ready to drop them in the trash.

*What did you think?* Dagmar asked.

I held onto my shoes and smiled. *When can we do it again?*

On the first Sunday of every month, I pulled out my calling card and dialed home. I told Mom about our trip to the North Sea.

"Quite an adventure, son," she said, then coughed.

"Have you been to the doctor?" I asked, even though I knew the answer. She never went to the doctor. I was lucky if I found an aspirin or a band-aid in the medicine cabinet when I needed one.

"It's not worth the trip," she said. "I'm around sick people all the time. I pick up their junk every once in a while."

I waited a moment, then said, "I've been thinking—" I could almost hear her mind saying, *Now what?* "About maybe staying—and finishing school here."

"But I thought that's what you were doing," she said. "Isn't it over in July?"

I wound the cord around my finger. "I mean—finishing high school." There was a long pause. I heard the echo of my own voice reaching her.

"That family has already done enough for you," she said. "You can't ask them to take you on for another year."

The phone was on a table in the hallway next to the kitchen. Even though the Trägers spoke a little English, I knew they weren't listening. They were caught up in their own Sunday night activities—laundry, TV, reading.

"I've thought about that, Mom," I said. "I'll be old enough to work here. I can get a job and either pay them rent or I can rent a room somewhere else."

She exhaled. "Have you talked to them about it?"

"No," I said. "I wanted to talk to you first."

Later that night, as we all ate our Sunday night dinner of open-faced sandwiches, Dagmar asked me how my mom was.

*She's okay*, I said. *She has a cold that won't go away.* I cut a huge bite of sandwich with my fork and knife. *I mentioned something to her about staying in Germany to finish high school and she didn't think it was a good idea, but I told her I'd get a job to pay for a room.* I shoved the bite of food in my mouth and chewed.

*Pay for a room where?* asked Dagmar.

I shrugged. *Wherever I can find one.*

Quatsch, she said. *You know you can stay here.*

I wiped my mouth with my napkin. *You've all done so much for me. I couldn't ask any more of you.*

She gave Helmut a look like *What do you think?* and he responded with a look of his own. *Possibly.*

Once a week Lars and I gave Blume a bath and scrub behind the ears. When she heard us coming, she scraped a hoof against the wood of her stall door, as if she had an internal clock with an alarm set for her bath. She didn't hoof the stall when we came to feed her. Only for bath.

I tossed soapy water over her back and at her ribs and Lars scrubbed in quick circles with the brush. Blume shuddered her hide close to where he touched, while I washed her mane—wetting it, rubbing it between my palms, squeezing out the soapy water in my fist, combing it with my fingers. Then Lars used a tool to scrape out the dried mud from her hooves. After we finished, she pranced around the pasture with her head tilted, shaking her mane. She knew she looked pretty.

*Want to try again?* Lars pointed at Blume with his head.

*No,* I said. *Once was enough.*

*But she was so easy with you,* said Lars.

*I know,* I said. *I don't want to press my luck.*

Blume stretched her neck through the fence rail to reach a patch of wildflowers. She wound her tongue around some stems, pulled, and chomped them with her back teeth.

*Besides,* I said. *She's your horse. She only wants you to guide her.*

*Du spinnt,* said Lars, shaking an open hand in front of his face, the German version of circling a finger next to your temple.

Karsten was happy I finally asked him for help with something. He researched exactly what I needed to do to get a work permit, then he brought me an application to fill out. One day after school, we rode our bikes to a building just outside the city center and went inside.

*I give them the application and then, what? They give me the permit?* I asked as we locked our bikes.

Karsten smiled at this. *You have a lot to learn.*

We waited in line a couple of hours, at which time, I handed the clerk my application, she stamped it and said I'd receive the paperwork in the mail.

*How long will it take to get the permit in the mail?* I asked Karsten.

*Oh, they aren't sending you the permit,* he said. *They're sending you the permission to apply for a permit.*

*I thought that's what I just did,* I said.

He held the door open for me. *No, you filled out the request for permission. They're sending you their approval—you hope—then you can fill out the permit application. After that, more waiting in lines.* We unlocked our bikes. *You'll see—we Germans love procedure.*

Herr Keller insisted I audition for the Heidelberg Madrigal Choir. The director, he said, was also the director and head instructor of choir at the Mannheim Music School. If I won a spot with the Heidelberg Choir, I would almost be guaranteed to study at Mannheim after high school. Herr Keller was two steps ahead of me. I was focused on finishing this school year and possibly staying for another. Never had I entertained the idea of continuing on through university. But I went along with Keller because why not? It was good experience. And if I decided to leave, in June or a year later, it could only help with college applications in the US.

He took the audition more seriously than I did. To me, the Madrigal Choir was extracurricular, a bonus. To him, whether we succeeded or failed was on the line. He had been torn about which song to choose for the audition. The song they'd ask me to sing would surely be in German, but what about my own selection? For weeks, we'd practiced Bach's "Sanctus in D Major," which was in Latin. Herr Keller felt it was a safe choice, neither German nor English, but then he'd suddenly switched the week before the audition to wanting a deeply American song.

*So long as it isn't* "Somewhere Over the Rainbow," I said to him. *Everyone uses that song. It's audition cliché and almost guarantees a no.*

"Somewhere Over the Rainbow!" *That's perfect! They may over-use it in America, but not here.*

*No.*

*Why not?*

*It's tryout cliché, kitsch.*

*We Germans invented kitsch. They'll eat it up.*

*No.*

He pushed for Copland. As far as Keller was concerned, Copland was America's only composer worth a damn and I must show them the unique voice I would bring to the choir. He pushed for "The Boatmen's Dance," part of Copland's Old American Songs.

It fit my voice exactly. But Keller wanted me to play with the song. Dance a little, drag out words as if I were at a honky-tonk. I refused and sang it straight, which frustrated him and around we went.

*Again*, he said.

"High row the boatman row, floatin' down the river. The Ohio."

*No*, he said. *Not the o-HI-o. The O-hi-O. Stress on the O's.*

*Not both O's. Just the first.*

*Both!*

*I think I know how to pronounce Ohio.*

*This is for a song. Follow the notes on the page.* He shook the sheet music in my face. *Again.*

I began to sing. He interrupted me.

*Wrong. Start again.*

I sang two notes.

*Wrong. Again.*

I wanted to leave. Why was I there? The audition seemed more for him than me. I started again.

*Wrong—*

*What do you want from me!* I shouted. *Perfection?*

*What else is there?*

We stared at each other.

*Failure. There is perfection and there is failure. Nothing between.*

*Then I fail.* I picked up my jacket and walked toward the door.

*You're going to throw everything away because you're angry? Stop being a child.*

I hesitated at the door. Then I said, *I want a different song.*

*You can't switch now. We only have two days.*

*I will only do the audition if it's a different song.*

He paused, grappling with whether to give in or not. *Which?*

"They Call the Wind Maria."

*I don't know this one.*

*I do.*

*Then sing it for me.*

I turned around and sang.

Helmut's family came to the Trägers for Easter. The men and children chattered while the women rushed in and out of the kitchen. Dagmar and the aunts put the last bowl in place and called us to the table. We sat and began passing the food. Ham wrapped in thin beef, roasted vegetables. When Lars passed me a bowl of gelatinous tennis balls, I stared.

*What's the matter, Yulli?* asked an aunt.

I looked at her, then Dagmar. *What is it?*

Kartoffelklöss, said Dagmar.

*Potato?* Now the whole table was staring at me. The hairs on the back of my neck rose.

*Yes*, said Dagmar. *Eat, Yulli, and stop asking so many questions.*

Everyone at the table had begun slipping forks of food into their mouths, so I did, too. The potatoes were like wallpaper paste.

*Yulli*, said the aunt who'd spoken earlier, *You have to eat them with gravy.* She held the gravy bowl toward me. I poured it on and had to admit, it did help.

*After lunch*, said Lars. *We play soccer.*

*With the* Kartoffelklösse? I said. That got a round of laughs.

"Ha, ha," said Lars. "You are the funny guy."

I shrugged, satisfied we were no longer talking about soccer.

At the head of the table sat Opa Träger. He was a jolly sort of man. Wiry, but with those rosy cheeks that'd made their way to Lars. Everything about my own grandpa seemed so heavy—the way he walked, how his hand thudded on the table as he finished a mouthful of food. But then, when we'd marched in parades together, him with his veteran buddies, me with the high school band, I was surprised at how light his steps were. And when I saw him, the pride I felt, as if I'd inherited his Purple Heart, like the ruddy cheeks passed down from Träger to Träger. And then I looked at Opa Träger—

*Opa Träger*, I spoke up so he could hear me. *Were you a soldier in the war?*

Everyone froze. Forks held in the air, mouths full of unchewed food, total silence.

I'd been to Dachau with the Trägers. Before we reached the *Arbeit Macht Frei* sign that slapped us in the face, we passed a Gypsy tent city.

*What are they doing here?* I asked. In Heidelberg, the Gypsies and Turks begged on the cobbled streets, usually with a young child as the point person while they sat some distance away. Once I saw a Gypsy child defecating on a cobbled street and his mother pointing at him with both hands then lifting them, palms up, to say, *You see? You see what you've reduced us to?* Another time I saw a woman, white-gloved hand shaking with age, kneeling, face deep inside a scarf. A man pressed a mark into her hand and, as she moved to put it in her pocket, I caught a glimpse of the unlined face of a teenager.

*They're protesting*, said Dagmar.

*Protesting what?*

*A new immigration law passed that doesn't favor the Turks*, said Helmut. *But they're on this land specifically because they're protected here. They can't be kicked off.*

We passed through the gate and under the sign. I pointed at a huge sculpture. *What is that? Barbed wire?*

As we approached I realized it was a tangle of black iron skeletons. We stood in front of it for a while, then walked the perimeter. All the silence was making me uncomfortable.

*Well*, I said. *I would have done okay here.* I grabbed a handful of belly. *All this fat.* I laughed and Lars did, too.

*Boys!* said Dagmar. *Behave yourselves. This is not the place to laugh and joke. Think beyond the ends of your own noses.*

Our laughter trailed off a little at a time and stopped after the second death stare from Dagmar. Lars and I put his parents between us. Then we stepped inside the barracks and the quiet moved through us and stopped in our throats.

The silence that followed my question to Opa Träger underlined how loud I'd spoken. My ears stung with embarrassment.

Opa Träger squinted an eye, held his hand to an ear sprouting gray hair and asked *How, please?*

Mumbles of *too young* smattered throughout the chairs.

Lars said, *Can't you see, Yulli? He was too young.*

Helmut told Opa Träger I'd asked if his food tasted good.

Jawohl, said Opa Träger.

I forced myself to look at Helmut. He nodded and told me without speaking, *Everyone makes mistakes.*

*Come on, Yulli. We need a fourth person.* Lars rolled a soccer ball under his foot. His two cousins waited for my answer.

*But I don't know how to play,* I said. *What about your other cousin?* I pointed to her.

*She's two,* said Lars, annoyed. *It's not difficult. You just kick the ball.*

The four of us walked toward the pasture.

*What about the manure?* I asked.

Lars smiled. *That's part of the fun.*

Blume was out of her stall. I went to her and ran a hand between her eyes. She shook her mane.

*Come on, Blume.* Lars led her into her stall. *You might trip. Or get hit with the ball.*

The cousins waited for Lars to return with instructions. This was obviously nothing new—Lars running the show. *Your goal is between these two posts,* he said. *Yulli and I will guard between those.* He pointed out our goalposts as he passed the ball from knee to knee. *Martin, you kick off.* He bounced the ball off his ankle toward Martin.

Lars brought me close to him. *All I need you to do is guard the goal. I can take on Martin and Hanna, no problem.*

I asked again about the goalposts and he stood between them, arms spread to show what an easy time I'd have. Martin kicked off and I squatted in anticipation of the ball coming toward me, but as time went on I stood higher and higher till I was upright picking at the long grass next to the goals. Lars kept the game on their side of the pasture. I pulled a weed apart, humming a warm-up exercise.

The ball hit the post next to me so hard I jumped.

*Wake up, Yulli*, said Lars. The three cousins laughed.

*Thank God you have good aim*, I said to Lars. *That could have hurt.*

*Being a goalie isn't easy*, said Lars. *You have to pay attention at all times. And usually the ball comes at you just like that.*

They moved again to the other side of the pasture. I watched for as long as I could, then my eyes got tired. *Lars*, I shouted. *I'm going in. You don't need me.*

*Come on.* He jogged toward me. *Let them kick a couple goals. I'll help you guard.* He waved them toward us.

He lined up the ball, stood behind it, rocked a couple times back and forth on his feet, took a couple steps, and kicked. I pulled myself in tight and moved out of the way. The ball bounced off the fence.

*Goal!* Lars raised his arms. *Okay, Yulli, this time, they're going to kick and you block.*

Hanna kicked first and I stuck my hand out, but the ball went wide. Martin's kick connected with my hip.

*Hey, Yulli*, said Lars. *Good block!*

*Now I'm really finished.* I left the goal box and walked toward the gate, rubbing my hip. I looked toward the stall and saw Blume with her nose in her feed pail. She raised her head and watched me while she chewed. She twitched an ear.

I felt a punch to my back and all the wind went out of my lungs. I was on the ground eye to eye with a pile of manure. I stayed there for a while struggling to catch my breath. Hanna came over to me.

*Are you okay, Yulli?*

*Yes*, I said. *I just need a moment.* I sat up, got to my knees then pushed myself off the ground. Martin and Lars passed the ball between them.

*Are you okay, Yulli?* asked Lars without looking at me.

*What happened?* I asked Hanna.

*Lars kicked the ball to you, but you didn't see and it hit you in the back.*

I looked over my shoulder and saw a smear of manure just below the blade.

At my next lesson, I told Herr Keller I'd applied for a work permit and asked if he had any ideas as to where I could find a job. He scribbled an address on a piece of paper and said, *Ask for Ingo.*

I pulled out the map I kept in my backpack and studied the index, then the web of streets until I finally located it, a street so tiny, the name barely fit, even in the smallest font.

I parked my bike in front of *Ingo's Musik* and immediately began to picture how I'd help kids find the right instrument to fit their personality. I imagined myself at the piano demonstrating scales with Liberace-esque mastery. The customers would buy a piano on the spot.

I went inside and loved that it smelled of wood and resin, that the floors creaked and the register was the old kind with push buttons and a bell.

Moin, Moin, I said to the sales clerk. *I take music lessons with Herr Keller. He said I should talk to Ingo about possibly working here.*

The clerk looked at me for a long time.

*We don't have any jobs for people like you*, he said.

My nose tingled and I actually sneezed. *You mean*—I sneezed again—*because I'm fat?*

A short, hairy man whose gray beard had neat, defined borders came through the curtain that I presumed led to the stockroom.

*No.* He stared straight through me. *I mean because you're homosexual.*

The bearded guy smacked the sales clerk, who barely flinched.

*Idiot,* said the bearded guy. *Homosexuals do good work.* Then he looked at me, *Very neat. Isn't that right?*

I stammered a Jawohl.

*You help me with repairs,* he said.


At the audition, I sweat a drip ring around myself.

*It's true you can sing,* said Professor Kegelmann in an almost bored voice. *However, I don't want to offer you a spot and incorporate you into the program only to have you leave in a few months.*

I pulled a handkerchief from my pocket and cleared my brow. *I plan to stay through the following school year,* I said. *After that, it depends on whether I can find placement at a music school.*

Professor Kegelmann cracked a smile. *I might know someone who can help you with that.*

The others sitting by him laughed.

*That will be all,* he said to me.

I gave a quick nod and left the room.


That evening as I was washing dishes with Dagmar, she said since I was going to stay another year, I should have a proper bed.

*I'll take you shopping this weekend.*

*You don't need to do that. I'm fine with the bed I have.*

*We had another exchange student a couple of years ago.* She circled the face of a plate with her towel and set it atop the stack in the cupboard. *She was from Argentina. You know, a lot of Germans went there after the war.*

I didn't, but I said yes anyway.

*Her grandparents were German—that's why she wanted to study here.* She picked up a handful of silverware and started drying. *We prepared everything, gave the bed you have to my sister and bought a new one. The girl flew back to Argentina two weeks after arriving.* Dagmar stopped drying. *That's why we never bought you a proper bed.*

I set a glass in the cupboard. *Where's the bed you bought for her?*

*At my sister's,* she said.

*You could just swap again.*

*She will be so annoyed,* said Dagmar. *But, yes, you're right.* She folded her towel. *And I do like to annoy my sister.*

I considered never going back to Ingo's, but my need for cash was stronger than my fear of the clerk. I arrived early the day I was told to begin work. The clerk looked up from his newspaper and pointed me toward the back with his head, then returned to his reading.

I followed the sound of a radio and found the man in the back replacing the pads on the keys of a clarinet.

I offered my hand. *Ingo? I'm Yulli.*

He continued with his work. *Ingo is dead. He was my brother and I never bothered changing the sign.* He looked up. *What kind of name is Yulli?*

I blushed. *It's a nickname.*

*People with nicknames usually want to fill up the air with chatter, constantly talking, uncomfortable with quiet.* He went back to his work. *I like quiet.*

I pulled my paperwork out of my jacket pocket. *I have my work permit and other documents.*

*Good, good,* he said. *But right now I have a French horn that needs cleaning and maintenance. No time to waste.*

The Heidelberg Madrigal Choir had started giving concerts at the castle the year before I joined. In preparation for our upcoming concert, Professor Kegelmann wanted to practice outdoors to get a handle on the acoustics. He decided we'd practice one evening at the Thingstätte, an amphitheater built in 1934 atop a mountain among Roman and Celtic ruins. The day the amphitheater opened in 1935, twenty thousand people turned out to hear Joseph Goebbels, the driving force and architect behind the Thingstätte, deliver a speech.

The amphitheater was abandoned after the war and had been converted to a park. When we went there to practice, it was near dusk and only three people sat on the weather-worn stone benches. After we finished the first song, the tiny audience clapped. The performance at the castle was to be held in about a month, five days before my return flight to America, which I hadn't changed yet. I was still deciding whether to go home for a month and return or stay in Heidelberg without a trip home. I had just enough money to switch the ticket; however, I would need every cent I earned later to pay for an apartment.

At dinner one night, Helmut pulled an envelope from his front shirt pocket.

*Yulli*, said Helmut. *This is for you.*

Dagmar and Lars were curious. Whatever was inside the envelope was a surprise to them, too. I opened it.

*Two tickets*, I said.

*For the German Chamber Philharmonic.* Helmut was pleased with his surprise. *I wanted you to see an opera, but the season is over. The Stuttgart Chamber Choir will be there to perform Mendelssohn's "St. Paul."*

*Why only two tickets?* asked Lars. *Who's going?*

*Yulli and I. You have a soccer game that night.*

*I can miss it*, said Lars.

Dagmar spooned celeriac soup into our bowls.

*We'd have to sit separate at this point*, said Helmut. *The show is in four days so there weren't many tickets left.*

*Thank you*, I said, still staring at the tickets. *Lars, if you really want to go, you can have my ticket and I'll go some other time.*

Quatsch, said Helmut. *It's your birthday present.*

My birthday wasn't for another week. I had forgotten all about it.

*We'll have fun at soccer, Lars*, said Dagmar. *Afterwards, we'll stop for ice cream at the place with the huge sundaes.*

Super geil, said Lars, monotone, cheek in his palm.

The concert was an education. I'd been practicing all this time, focused on hitting the right notes, grappling with precision, the length of each breath. But to sing better, all I had to do was close my eyes and feel the vibration of my own voice. Because when a choir like Stuttgart's performs, you come to understand music is about the transference of energy. In order to lift someone else up, you must first lift up yourself. To know that my voice could cause a shift inside another person was magic.

During intermission, Helmut bought two beers and we stood at a high table. He asked about my life back home. I told him my hometown was in an area called the Great Black Swamp. In the mid 1800s, the German settlers came and broke their backs digging ditches to drain it, then died from malaria in swarms. The church in the next town over, Darmstadt, is a replica of the one in Darmstadt, Germany. Across the street is a graveyard where the stones have been removed from individual graves and arranged into a tiered arc, an altar of sorts. All the names and epitaphs on those stones are in German. And the town newspaper was printed in German until World War I, when it became apparent that all German heritage was best kept hidden.

*That's all very interesting,* said Helmut. *But what about your family?*

*I have a small family,* I said. *It's just my mom, my mom's dad, and me.* I drank a sip of beer. *My grandpa has diabetes. We moved in with him a couple years ago after he had an episode.*

*And, your father? What happened to him?*

*I happened to him,* I said with a laugh.

Helmut kept a serious face.

*I don't know where he is exactly,* I said. *Somewhere in Vietnam or Cambodia doctoring people who've stepped on mines. He left when I was a baby and told my mom he'd be back in a few months.* I scanned the crowd. People stood in clusters, carrying on conversations lighter than ours. *Whenever I think about him, I only see the back of him, never his face. I watch him step into the jungle and then the trees close behind him like a curtain and he's gone.*

Helmut took a drink. *You've never received a letter?*

I shook my head no.

*No postcard? Nothing?*

I focused on the couple in front of us, both wearing scarves tied in precise, yet effortless knots.

Helmut pulled the label off the beer bottle. *He panicked,* he said. *I know that panic.* He smoothed the label on the tablecloth. *When Lars was three weeks old, I left. I was overwhelmed. I packed a bag and stepped on a train and rode it till it stopped.*

I blinked again and again, as if to rid myself of the image. *Where did you go?*

*Italy,* he said. *Milan.*

I bit the inside of my cheek.

*I was there for about a month,* he said. *Then one night, I was in a bar with a woman and I looked at her and thought, What am I doing here? So I told her I was going to the bathroom and left for the train station.* He pressed his lips together. *It took me that long to learn only boys go on adventures never to return. And I wasn't a boy anymore.*

I took a moment to absorb this new version of Helmut, then said, *Dagmar was okay with you coming back?*

*Oh, no,* he said. *You know her. No nonsense. She wouldn't let me in the house for a long time, months maybe. But I won her over.*

The lights in the hall flashed, telling us to return to our seats.

*How?*

*I apologized—a lot. I told her what I said to you, that I left a boy and returned a man.* He finished his beer. *And I promised that once a boy steps over the line into manhood, he can never cross back.*

*Do you believe that?*

*I'm not sure. But I will say—I've never been back to Italy.*

*Do you think you'll ever go again?*

*Yes, but only when Dagmar's ready.*

A week later, Lars and Helmut loaded Blume into her trailer and I joined them for a trip to the country. Blume needed to be re-shoed, then Lars was scheduled for a test with his riding instructor. He'd been practicing maneuvers all week, changing pace, moving left, then right, then left again on command, jumping low obstacles.

Lars threaded the metal bar of the bit between Blume's teeth, which, once in place, she chewed as if it were a bunch of hay. He led her out of the stall and dropped her off for shoeing then we went to the indoor ring so Lars could watch another rider's test.

*How was soccer, Lars?* I asked.

*I scored a goal and blocked another from going in.*

When we reached the railing he stepped onto the bottom rung to get a better view.

*Next month*, said Helmut, *You, your mother, and I are going to the opera.*

*I don't know. It sounds boring to me.*

*Oh, no*, I said. *Next month it'll be in German. And, you'll love—*

*Papa? Do you see how the rider keeps her upper body still during a jump?*

Ja, ja, said Helmut.

Then they fell into conversation about how Lars should approach the jump. Lars was pretty confident going in to the test, but Blume trotted left when he wanted her to move right, then, a little while later, she stopped mid-canter to launch a waterfall of urine into the dirt. The test ended with her refusing the jump.

*I wanted to pass that test so I could start Reining*, said Lars afterwards. His cheeks were high pink with anger.

*We'll schedule you for another test next week*, said Helmut. *It'll only be a week delay.*

*But I wanted the test over with.* He flung his helmet against Blume's stall.

*Pick that up*, said Helmut.

Lars didn't move.

*Now.* It was the only time I saw Helmut lose his temper.

Lars snatched the helmet from the dirt and brushed it off.

*I'm going inside to pay dues*, said Helmut. *Get in some practice time while you're here.* He turned and left.

Lars watched him go, then clicked his tongue and led Blume in the direction of the outdoor practice ring. *Come on, then*, he said to me.

Beyond the outdoor ring were pastures with tall wildflowers and a path that meandered toward the woods then disappeared. When we got to the ring, I stopped at the fence.

*Come in*, said Lars.

*Why?*

*You should ride her again.*

I didn't move. *Your dad said you needed to practice.*

*She needs the practice, not me.*

*Don't you both need the practice?*

Lars waved me toward them.

*But—she's tired and could use a rest.*

Quatsch, he said. *She's a horse. She wants to be out trotting the fence line.*

*You know I'm not very good at this*, I told him as I approached. *Maybe you should ride her first*, I said.

He gave her quivering flesh a few slaps down the length of her. *This is the best time to ride*, he said. *When she's already got her energy out.* He took off his jacket and hung it on a post.

I felt like I owed him for spending time with his dad. His dad, not mine. *Okay*, I said.

*You remember how to get up there?*

*Maybe you should show me.*

*You don't need me to*, he said. Blume's nostrils opened and closed as he tightened the saddle.

It took me a few tries, but I finally made it to the top of Blume's saddle. Lars threaded a rope through the end of Blume's bit and led us slowly across the ring and back. He stood and had her walk in a tight circle around him, letting out the rope a little at a time. Then he brought her to a trot.

*That's fast enough.* I squeezed my knees to her ribs.

Lars clicked his tongue and Blume moved into a gallop.

I gripped the reins tighter. *Slower!* I yelled.

He clicked his tongue again. She moved faster. I couldn't see beyond the end of Blume. I couldn't yell at Lars to stop. I concentrated on the saddle. If I got off this horse, I promised myself, I'd never get on another.

"Blume?" I said just loud enough for her to hear. "Don't listen to him. Slow down, Blume."

She kept going. The pull against her bit was annoying her, and she began to yank her head to one side, away from Lars. Then he must have let go of the rope because she ran directly toward the fence. I held tight with the reins in my fists and my thighs death-vicing the saddle. I thought about launching sideways off her, but there wasn't time. And there was also the fence. She broke stride long enough to push off the ground and flew over the top rail. We came down with a smack and I pulled on her reins, which was a mistake because she bucked, front two legs pedaling the air. I know I was screaming, and if I wouldn't have been the one in my predicament, I'd have found it equal parts frightening and hilarious. She dropped her hooves to the ground and bolted toward the tree line. By that time, I'd given up. She was going where she wanted and my job wasn't to guide her—it was to stay on.

She kept pace all the way to the trees and I started to shout, "Whoa! Whoa! Stop, Blume, Stop!" because I knew there was no way I'd make it out in one piece on the other side of the woods. I expected her to lose speed a little at a time, but, just before the tree line, she stopped. I kept going. I was in tall grass rolling like a log downhill. I slammed into something—what, I didn't know. I opened my eyes and looked up at the glints of sky coming through a swath of leaves. Blume stood a few feet from me munching on wildflowers, swishing her tail. My shoulder began to tingle, then stabs of pain spiked down to my fingertips.

I heard Lars shouting my name from afar. I sat up and rubbed my arm. There would be a bruise, but I could lift my arm and move it.

Lars ran to me, wild-eyed and smiling. *Yulli*, he said. *You're crazy. Why did you stay on her?*

*What do you mean?* I said. *What else was I supposed to do?*

*Jump off, of course.*

*Jump off where?* I winced and grabbed my shoulder. *Headfirst into the fence?*

*To the side.* Lars held out a hand to help me up. *Are you okay?*

I shooed him away and moved to my knees then stood. *I don't know*, I said. *Why'd you do that?*

*Do what?* He grabbed Blume's bit and started walking her back toward the stables.

*Do what*, I said, *as if you don't know.*

*Horses can sense when you are scared*, he said. *You have to lead them.* He stopped and waited for me to catch up.

*I can't lead a horse. I barely know how to ride one.*

He smiled. *Yeah, but what a ride it was.*

*Not funny*, I said.

*But, fun, though*, he said.

Du spinnt, I said and shook a hand in front of my face. *Don't ever do that to me again.*

*Okay, okay,* he said.

*I'm serious!* I shouted, which startled him. He'd never heard me raise my voice in anger.

*Okay, Yulli*, he said, quieter, as we left the forest.

At the edge of the Black Forest sits a town called Pforzheim. In early December, we'd gone to Pforzheim to visit Dagmar's sister. Lars and I took her dog for a walk and, at the end of her street, we followed a path into the forest. The trees were sparse at the start and

I was focused on the patterns of the frost-coated tree tips. Then all of a sudden I realized we had just stepped into *the* Black Forest. We approached a tower of some sort, which wasn't that high. Lars and I guessed it was simply a lookout. We tied the dog to a tree trunk and climbed the metal rungs to the platform.

Super geil, said Lars, in awe.

*Beautiful*, I said.

Our words hovered in the cold air a moment before disappearing. Bouquets of ice-glazed branches brushed the sky. Layer upon layer rippled toward the horizon. I knew then that the Black Forest really was magical, because every year it transforms itself into a bolt of intricate lace.

The night before I was to perform with the Madrigal Choir, I called my mom and told her I was ready to come home.

"For good?" she said.

"Yeah," I said. "I need to get back and start thinking about college."

"I'm glad to hear that." She coughed. "We miss you."

All I had to say to Dagmar was *Don't worry about switching the bed*, to which she nodded once and continued folding laundry. When I told Helmut about wanting to fly back to America as soon as school ended, he said he thought I was staying longer. They'd planned a trip to Holland.

*It's just my mom and grandpa at home*, I said. *They need me.*

*Then you must go.*

The next morning, I found Lars in the hallway on his stomach, legs bent at the knees and feet rocking back and forth in the air, drawing a tiger on graph paper.

*That's very good*, I said.

*It'll be better once I color it.*

I watched him erase a paw and start over. *Did your papa tell you that I'm leaving soon?*

*Yeah.* He bit his tongue with his side teeth as he drew the arc of a back leg.

*Okay*, I said. *I just wanted to make sure you knew.* I turned to go back to my room.

*Yulli?*

*Yes, Lars.*

*When will you return?*

*I don't know.*

He stopped drawing. *But you'll go to Gymnasium again next year?*

*No, Lars*, I said. *I have to finish school in America.*

*Oh.* He returned to his tiger.

*I'll come back as soon as I can.*

*Maybe I can come see you*, he said.

We looked at each other, then I said, *That would be* super geil.

I waited until after the concert to tell Professor Kegelmann it would be my only performance with the choir and that I was sorry. I realized I'd said I would stay, but I had to go home to my family. He said he understood and wished me well and that was that.

Herr Keller was angry at first.

*You're throwing away all this work and effort?* he said.

*No*, I said. *I plan to study music at a university in America. And thanks to you and the choir, I already have a huge advantage over other students. How many American students can say they've sung in a European choir?*

*You're making a mistake*, he said.

*Probably*, I said. *But only boys go on adventures never to return.*

*What a pile of shit*, he said. *Who do you think settled America?*

*Boys? No. Men—and women. That's the real sacrifice, never going back.* He gathered his things and left the practice room.

The night before I left, I met Karsten and his new girlfriend, Nadine, at a bar called the Ratskeller.

Karsten gave me a hug and a few hearty slaps on the back. *I had fun things planned for this summer. A bike trip and camping, all the way to Holland!*

*That sounds—terrible.*

We all laughed. Then I said, *But I would've gone anyway.* We sipped our beers and an awkwardness set in, so I felt it was my job to break it. *I'm sorry I wasted your time with all the permit stuff.*

*It wasn't a waste. Now I know exactly what to do when the next exchange student decides to stay,* he said. *There's always one.* We smiled and Karsten put an arm around Nadine.

The music started. It was so loud we danced and drank instead of talking, which is, I think, how we preferred it. Who wants to hear goodbye?

Then one moment I looked up and saw Herr Keller and Ingo's brother, whose name I eventually learned was Fred, coming toward me.

*What are you guys doing here?* I shouted.

*We heard there was a party,* said Herr Keller, smiling.

*How?*

Herr Keller pointed his thumb at Karsten.

*I thought you liked quiet,* I said to Fred.

He tilted his head back and forth. *Only when I'm working.*

They went to get beers and, when they returned, Herr Keller clapped me on the shoulder and said, *You're a good kid* and that was the last I saw of them. They went off into the crowd and probably finished their beers and left because I never found them again.

After last call, the music died down and an oompah band parted the crowd. The tuba player led the mini-parade, followed by the accordion player, the clarinet, and a woman dressed in a fluorescent clown outfit. As she walked she tossed handfuls of rainbow confetti on the crowd. Bright green and pink dots clung to the wispy hairs of the tuba player's moustache. The band knew they were a cliché and didn't care. Neither did the rest of us. We all smiled with our fluorescent teeth and opened our hands to the confetti making drifts on our shoulders.

The Trägers walked me to my gate at the airport, carrying all of my things despite my protests. When my flight was announced over the loudspeaker, I felt like I'd been cemented to the chair.

*Looks like it's your turn*, said Helmut. He stood and the rest of the family followed. I was last to stand.

Dagmar hugged me. She kissed me on the cheek and told me my mother would be happy to see me. She wiped away tears with the knuckle of her thumb. Helmut gave me a few slaps on my shoulder and a hug. *Keep studying your music*, he said.

We all stood in a circle, not wanting to be the first to break it. *Goodbye, Lars.*

He nearly tackled me into my seat. I had to plant my feet into the ground to keep the pair of us from falling.

He let go and asked, *What will you do without us?*

I laughed and held myself tight to keep from crying.

*You'll just have to come back next year*, he said.

*That would be nice.* I messed his curls. *I'll miss you, Lars.*

*Of course you will*, he said.

On the day I arrived, I'd approached Helmut first. "Guten Tag," I said and pointed at the sign he was holding, then at my own chest.

"Chew-lian?" said Dagmar, unsure of her pronunciation.

"Julian," I said.

After a few minutes, it became apparent my name was a struggle for them, like an oversized bite of food in their mouths. In my rudimentary German, I told them, if they'd like, they could pronounce my name Yulian. Or even Yulli. Which sounds like "July" in German.

*July?* Lars said. Then his eyes widened, as if he had just remembered a lost thought. *In Germany, you become a month of summer.*

The Trägers and I exchanged letters at Christmas for a while, then those trailed off, as things do in life. I searched for them online a few times, but to no avail. The past couple of years, I have written them a letter at Christmas, but I can never bring myself to send it. What if they've moved and I find the letter marked *Return to Sender* in my mailbox? I'd rather go on believing they're content in their house eating plum cake and drinking tea while Blume pulls wildflowers through the fence posts of her pasture across the street.

As for me, I went on to study music at Baldwin Wallace. My mom's never-ending cold was diagnosed as leukemia and Grandpa's health took a sharp dive during my first year of college. It was a difficult time that required I spend six years in college instead of four. Grandpa's death hit me hard because then it was just my mom and me, and how could I leave her alone? After college, I tried the professional opera route, but life got in the way. I had a sick mother to care for and couldn't fly across the country at the drop of a hat for auditions. Besides, a career as a professional opera singer is a tough gig for those who don't have huge reputations.

But right now, the show's about to begin. Backstage, I have my own table in a quiet corner. I decorated my space with pictures of the love of my life, Ruben, and the friends and family we've made together. There's a picture of me conducting my first group of students at their spring choir performance. And a few portraits of those who aren't here, but who helped me earn my moment in the spotlight: my mom, my grandparents, my best college friend, and a family at an island picnic table just before crossing the muddy seabed to a faraway shore.